We All We Got

We All We Got

Me, My Brother, and My Cousin

Lyfe N' General

Library of Congress Control Number: 2010908112
ISBN: Hardcover   978-1-4535-1372-9
                Softcover   978-1-4535-1371-2

This book was printed in the United States of America.

To order additional copies of this book, contact:
Xlibris Corporation
1-888-795-4274
www.Xlibris.com
Orders@Xlibris.com
53996

CONTENTS

Thanks can be said and expressed in a million different ways.

But as I bring this project to a close for now; because there will be a follow up; *Part* 2 is soon to arrive. Until then, I have a whole lot of people that I would like to reach out and grab with my choice of words. First and foremost, let me send my first regards and say *thank you* to the Lord himself, because there is no me without him. Through him, I am everything, but without him I am nothing. Thanks to the strongest woman; I've ever encounter within these thirty years of living. My mother, I know I'm a hard pill to swallow at times, but that's life; and I am who I am, and not a day can pass me by with me not giving it all I got, to make u feel all things you've missed, trying your hardest to provide the best for all four of us. I love you is all I have to say. Now Crystal you know like I know; you my dear I love you without a second thought, Vanity, Linda and my Stinky Momma. I love all my girls. Anna Anna, Niaa, and my ZZ (Nikkia, you too) I love you too. A special thanks goes out to all my loved ones. Especially my one and only son, my trademark in this world. I know we've been through a lot, but we did it together, and that's all that really matters to me. I can't forget about all the people who believed in me, when there were a whole lot who could care less about me and mine. But that has always been my motivation to reach beyond my full limits. I wish I could let the world know how much I miss all my real niggas; niggaz that never really got a chance to reach out and touch the world with their unconditional love. *Rest* in *peace* to Tremaine Thomas; the brother I never had, but was always concerned about my well-being. My Ghetto Hero. RIP to Lil Wesley-Yoshima-Osman-Lil, E-Gary Duffey-G, Hicks-Robert, Levi-Pat, Troy-Mann, Thronton-Big dale-G, Wayne Trigger, and last but not least dat young nigga tra off dat Lottie blk. I miss all my niggaz that fell victim to these streets, even you boyz thats on lock. I want you all to know that these streets ain't the same out here. You have to search for new avenues and then the world is yours for the keeping. Big Tyrone-Popeye-Nigel from dem jects and the list goes on. But I shouldn't have to mention a few names, because they know who they are in my life and they also know how deep my love goes when it comes to my love for them. I'm a proven factor, all because I'm active in your life.

CHAPTER 1

We All We got

October 21, 2008

Texas weather was at an all-time scorching high; 101 degrees in the late part of October. The sun was shining, as a nice gentle breeze blew across the general population of the Federal Correctional Institution in Bastrop, Texas. A world within the world—as the sound of inmates holding conversations amongst one another, while standing in the commissary line, each individual waiting and listening for their name to be called over a loud intercom.

"Last call for Juan Lopez," the commissary correctional officer announced, as everyone looked around to see who was Juan Lopez, only to find a short, chubby, Hispanic male in high pursuit, in hope of being able to make store. Once he did arrive through the commissary doors, he was out of breath, denied, and turned around by the officer working.

"That's some bullshit, that hoe ass CO know he could've let ol' boy shop!" I said, as I shook my head in total disbelief, about how certain correctional officers make it their mission to treat the inmate population as being less than human being and then wonder why verbal attacks are so common in prison.

"Youngster, that's just the way life is, whenever you're on someone else's time," Pops began in his raspy tone of voice. "Because if he was at the right place at the right time, he wouldn't have had to worry about being denied like he was. He missed out on his golden opportunity. It's just that simple," Pops added, as we continued to stand in line and push past the fact that it was Juan's problem and not ours. Better luck next time.

"Youngster," Pops said catching my attention and bringing me back to our original conversation before we were interrupted by the everyday cycle of prison life.

"Back in my days, I was one of the few that ran the streets of Waco, Texas, that could get these hands on anything, rather it was an airplane or parts for train," Pops began, as he held his hands up high in the air as if they were on display in a museum.

"These are God's gift to man," he added as he reached out for my hand, for one of them old playa handshakes to seal his last statement. I couldn't help but to laugh, as he continued to fill me in about his day and era in the mid-1980s. In which, he did all the talking and I just listened, entertained, and amused, while he reminiscence about "The good old days," as he would call 'em.

"Youngster, I can still recall, that I was one of the first to ever come through Waco, Texas, in a 1984 convertible Corvette, cocaine white, with the tee-top sunroof, fresh off the showroom floor," Pops began with a smile engraved on his aging face, as he put his best foot forward and pulled up on his two-belt loops in true old playa fashion.

"That's when the Pioneer came out with a two-knob tape deck, and guess what I was bumping back then?"

"What's that, Pops?" I asked with a smirk on my face.

"That muthafucking Keith Sweat. His album had just came out, and this was back when you had to go to Dallas to buy the newest release, because Waco was always two or three weeks late, when it came to anything," Pops added, as he pulled out a white face towel from his back pocket and wiped the sweat off his forehead, before he began again.

"And plus this was back, before all that shoot'em up, bang-bang, hippy dee hop shit came about. This was back when it was cool to slow dance with your girl all night and go home and make love to baby, making music, when a person wouldn't get killed for stepping on another man's shoes on accident, that was when you could make over ten thousand dollars a night, standing in East Waco Park, right off hood street, and the laws didn't know every damn thang, not like they do now."

All I could do was agree with Pops, because I've heard a lot about those days, even though I was to young to be apart of his era, I wasn't too far behind his generation. I was more like a different chapter in the same book, but on a broader scale. Being a man who has had a long experience in the game, to Pops he was the uncle to all young hustlas. He either called us youngster or nephew. And that just depended on the moment, because at times, he might call you both of 'em.

"Nephew," he began in his raspy tone of voice, "I can still remember tha day I came through R. L. Smith Park, on one of them good old Sunday, where Bar-B-Que pits were fired up, kids was playing, music was jumping out the speakers, and I seen a concrete slab full of gambles, niggaz like Brick-Head, Ice-Man, Bone-Dick, Head-Bone, and some more muthafuckers. I parked my Vet on the green grass, stepped out, tilted my cream-colored Dobbs hat to the side, and pointed my three-inch square toe alligators and headed straight to the sight of money," Pops continued as the memory seemed like it lifted his spirits, just thinking about it.

"It was a young playa that went by the name of Lil' Daddy shooting the dice when I walked up, and when he seen me; he yelled out Big Poppa two hundred dollars I shoot," Pops added, as he just stared laughing, like it tickled him to even retrieve these thoughts from his recollection.

I stood there entertained, waiting to hear what happened next, knowing he was about to deliver a mean punch-line.

"So what happened after that?" I asked.

"Shid, I picked up the dice to examine 'em and told that nigga to shoot everything he got."

"Na'll Pops, you ain't tell Lil' Daddy that, did you?" I emphasized ampping him up to elaborate on this "*hood tale.*"

"Shid, if I didn't, and the nigga called my bet thinking I was bluffing, when he counted out two thousand-two hundred-and thirty-nine dollars, that's all the nigga had to his name; as I counted out twenty-three fresh out-of-the-bank, crispy, one hundred-dollar bills and handed it to the houseman and told him to keep the change, as I rolled him back the dice. The nigga shook 'em and rolled his first roll, but I caught 'em and asked around the table, "Do anybody else like the dice." Nobody said a thang, so I let him shoot. "Nephew, that Nigga shook them dice and released 'em from his hands, causing them to tumble, hop, and then come to a complete stop ACE-DEUCE." I mean you should've seen these niggas faces as I gathered up all my money and pointed my three-inch square toes alligators straight to my Vet, with some of the quickest money I've ever made in this game of life"

Charles Bates, better known as Pops, has been in Federal Prison for the past sixteen years, for his part in one of the biggest drug trafficking conspiracies Waco, Texas, has ever seen. He's currently serving a life sentence, in which he'll spend the remaining of his life behind the steel curtain of these prison walls. To sit here and listen to him press rewind on his life; then press play on what's considered to be his highlighted moments was more of a reality check than anything to me. One bad decision and this could be anybody in this day and age. Here was a real good dude, who would give you his last if you needed it, trapped in the system paying his dues with his entire life, for the one mistake he made and became what the streets call a living legend.

(Chapter 2)

Young Pups on the Porch

August 11, 1992

"Nigga, shoot fifty cents." We heard a formal voice say, as me and my brother Dough-Boy pulled our bikes on the side of our aunt Dee's house.

"Mann, I'm shooting a dollar, you can't tell me what to shoot," Crazy Kev was saying, as they all looked up to see us walking up.

"What's up, cuddy?" Crazy Kev added, using the street terminology of cousin. In which, I've never known how that slang came about, but still to this day, it's part of the everyday language in Waco, Texas. It's like going to New Orleans and saying whoodie.

"What's up with you, boyz? I see ya'll got a good game going on," I began, as I squatted down in my dice shooting stand with three dollars in my hand, while sending my acknowledgments to my homeboys, Tip-Toe, Stinky, and Black Ty.

"Mann, shoot the dollar!" Tip-Toe said with a frown on his face, as he dropped a dollar bill on the blanket they were shooting dice on. Crazy Kev was pad rolling him out of all his money using the combinations along with the style that our uncle Pistol Pete had taught us all, but Crazy Kev was the only one who has perfected it all the way down to the tee. (All he ever did was sit around the house

13

with a blanket and a pair of dice practicing until he had it down to perfection.)

After we finished shooting dice, Crazy Kev was the winner again, counting his earnings of nineteen dollars.

"Look what I got," Tip-Toe pronounced as he held up a bag of weed, along with some rolling paper.

"That's what I'm talking about, fire it up," Dough-Boy said, as he pulled out a lighter from his front pocket. Me, knowing my brother, he was ready to start a fire somewhere; that was something just excited him, because he was infatuated with anything that consisted of danger.

"I would, but I'ma need a dollar from each one of ya'll," Tip-Toe explained.

"All, man, you gonna charge us to smoke," Stinky wined, because he was broke from the dice game. I can't believe this shit," he added. It was normal to hear him complaining about something. He was the oldest of us all, but we've all been homeboys since the beginning of time. We all grew up on the East Side, up until our moms moved us to the North Side, and we hated that shit with a passion. But that didn't stop us from making that bike ride with every chance we got, to get to the place we called "The Hood."

"Mann, I got to make some kind of money off this nigga. I stole this from my brother, so if he finds out, I'ma get an ass whopping, but before he do, I'ma make me five dollars off it," Tip-Toe added, hoping like hell he wouldn't have to face the repercussion for stealing from his big brother; in which, even when he did get caught, he'd take his ass whopping and still manage to do it again. His nickname fit him to the tee, because for one he walked on his tippy toes, and he was always creeping around like a burglar on the prowl, ready to steal somebody's shit. He was nominated for the best bike thief around town. He's been known to steal outfits hanging on clotheslines.

Like his momma would say, "Damn boy, will steal anything that ain't bolted down, and if was bolted down, he'd steal a power drill to unscrew the bolts and screws, and then pack it off." That was just him.

"Here, petty ass nigga," Crazy Kev began, as he dusted his knees off and handed Tip-Toe three dollars in quarters and two one dollar bills.

"Good, now, we can move forward," Tip-Toe added, as we all headed toward the outhouse in the backyard.

This was our getaway spot, a place where we sat up and cracked jokes on one another, shared our dreams of one day becoming rich with each other, and a place where we would smoke stolen cigarettes, whenever we could manage to find an abandoned pack just lying around our mother's house.

But today, we had some weed, and that meant we had to be extra careful. We couldn't get caught, because that meant an ass whopping on sight and about a month of punishment, where we can't leave our bedroom, so we had to be on our Ps and Qs.

"Hold up Dough-Boy, before you light it, let me fiund the incese first," Crazy Kev indicated, as he looked under a pile of winter clothes and pulled out a box of coconut smelling incense.

As we all took turns, in our routine of puff-puff-pass on each joint we smoke, and if one of us tried to get slick and get an extra puff, his ass got voted out on the next time the joint came around. Unlike Black Ty, this nigga always seemed to be the last one to hit everything. His title was the *Dope Dog* of the bunch.

"So Tear, you and Dough-Boy should be moving to Houston sometime soon, I hear," Stinky asked in a real drowsy tone of voice.

"Yea, mann, we should be gone in about two more days," I replied as I dropped my head and stared at the ground. "But we'll be back when schools out," I added, trying to shine light on the situation, because we really didn't want to move. Shid, we loved being in the midst of our homeboyz along with our favorite cousin, Crazy Kev.

We did everything together. What we have has grown from a friendship to a real form of brotherhood, next to a kinship. We all had each other's backs no matter what. People have always associated us with one another, because we were always together. Whenever you seen one, you seen at less two more with him, if not all five of us. That was just the way it was back then.

"I don't even know why we're moving anyway," Doughboy blurred out, sounding as if he had a chip on his shoulder.

"Nigga, you know why ya'll moving? Because yo' momma said so," Crazy Kev stated, as everybody burst out laughing, because it was one of those inside jokes, that we all played on each other; everyone except Black Ty, in which, we chose not to play with him like that due to the fact that his moms' was a crackhead who lived her life trapped in the cracks of the streets causing him to be in and out of juvenile hall or in foster care or living with different relatives who could care less about what he did or how he did it. Half the time, he was at my aunt Dee's house with Crazy Kev. He was treated like family, regardless of his present situation. He was welcomed to just walk in the house, eat, drink, take a shower, and do as if he was Crazy Kev. And through that, he was able to experience a true form of childhood love with a family that accepted him, as if he was one of their own.

He will never forget the day he turned eleven years old, one of his most passionate moments with this whole entire family; was when they all came together and threw him a real family big birthday bash, he got cards with money, gifts, cloths, and all the enjoyment of being a part of a special gathering. "All for me" was what ran through his mind that entire day. Everyone was there, except his own biological family and he had invited them all, but still a no show on their behalf. But it didn't faze him because to him that was normal. It was days like this that his life felt complete and he promised his self that he would keep it real with his family and live his life to the fullest, from here on out.

*   *   *

"I thought I said to be back in this damn house before eight o'clock." My momma had begun the moment we walked through the backdoor. "But here it is almost 9:30 p.m. and you two bring ya'll ass in this damn house as if I ain't said shit," she added as she continued to fold the shirt she had in her hands. We tried to avoid the confrontation, but ended up walking straight into it.

"We was playing basketball," I lied, trying to cover our tracks and sound sincere, all in the same motion.

"I don't want to hear it, just get in there and help Kaylon and Ry-Ry pack up them box's."

Linda Kay was a twenty-nine-year-old single mother of four, and she wanted a better life for her and her family. She knew her two oldest sons were so much like their father, when he was their age, that it hurt. All her kids are by a local drug dealer named Scotty-Boy; in which, he's serving 85 percent on a Federal 247 months sentence; at an United State Penitentiary in Atlanta, Georgia.

Tear was her oldest son, and he was fourteen years of age, always outgoing and charismatic, a real neat freak; and more of the sneaky type that avoided all forms of drama. Whereas her next to the oldest son, Dough-Boy, was two years younger than Tear and a total complete opposite, where Tear was tall, Dough-Boy was short, and whereas Dough-Boy was chubby, Tear was a skinny stick, but together, they made a complete package.

And Linda Kay felt like she had no other choice other than to move her family to a rest haven, to escape the pitfalls of the heart of the streets of Waco, Texas.

To her, Waco was a trap, and she wanted by all means to prevent her kids from falling victim to the system of collect calls, twenty-minute visits, or expensive ass-mailing stamps. So Houston was her best opinion, in that way she'd be able to advice in the real estate field and become an agent of some sort.

Tear was coming of age, and only time could tell when he'd get his hands on some of that illegal money. The kind that comes with all types of strings attached to it. And it's only obvious that his brother follow in his footsteps, along with his nephew Crazy Kev. Needless to say, but he was their right-hand man, and they all stuck tight like glue.

She didn't want either one of them to end up in prison, like their fathers "or" like their uncles "or" their oldest cousin, who would have to be labeled as their Ghetto Hero, because they all looked up to him and his was the only male figure to teach to be Young Hogz by knowing how to keep your chin up and chest out, The life line to the HILLTOP BLOODLINE; a role model indeed. In which, he was locked up too, doing state time for a murder. So she understood their connection, they were all family. She grew up in a large family of eleven herself, and all she wanted was to pursue her dreams and guide her family in the right direction, away from a place she knew too well, East Waco, Texas.

CHAPTER 3

Back to Bastrop

"So Pops, whatever happen' to all them hoes you had in your stable," I asked.

Entertained by his style of character, because Pops had a way of telling a story with very large indefinite quantity and graphics in his body movement, using words that rhythm to highlight each and every statement that he has made. In prison, you have a whole lot of old playaz that took the quickest route to the fastest cash.

And Pops was one of those dudes. A real certified flatfoot hustla, whose resume can cover the Las Vegas spread in the art of hustling. A drug dealer, a pimp, a pool shark, a card shark, and a pad roller wrapped all up in one forming, *A Real Streets Entrepreneur.* His motto was that "A playa can never be a day late 'or' a dollar short, because money will always be on time."

In a world where a person has to comprehend and adapt to their environment, it's easy for a child to be born and then grow up and become a Pops. Sad to say, but when you grow up without cable television to watch 'or' Nintendo games to play, all your entertainment is subject to come from the underworld, where your action figures are real humans that you aim to be when you come of age, and sometimes, you're forced to grow up faster than you want to.

"Mann, nephew, you know how that old saying goes; out of sight, out of mind," Pops began, "But you know I kept a fleet of bitches, in all shapes and sizes, in excellent running condition," he replied, as he grabbed his hat and crocked it to the side, bending the rim of it.

"Whatever happen' to that Ginger?"

"My snow bunny, boy, it's been years since I've even thought about ol' Ginger," he added, as he wiped his head with his face towel again, "Boy, how you remember her?"

"I just remember seeing her with you a lot, and plus, she gave me a dollar one time."

"Yea, so you got one of my hoes to rob Peter to pay Paul. Boy, I knew you had pimp potential," he added with a smile written on his face. "Nephew, that was one of my best pieces of bait right there. I can still remember the day I knocked ol' Ginger down in San Diego. I had about twelve flavors in my stable, baby. If you named it, I had it," Pops added, as he glanced at the sky and drifted off back down memory lane.

"I had come across these two pimp niggas, Big Whitt and Ice-Cream Slim, at this playa's convention in Chicago back in 1979, and they were both telling me about a hoe stroll they had been working and running hoes on, selling pussy out of both pants legs. At first, I was against it, but I was observing these niggas, dressed in chinchilla mink furs, diamonds glistening as the ice was turning colors, as they sat on the hood of Ice-Cream Slim's Benz 190, so I just said fuck it, nephew," Pops explained, as I stood there zoned in on this one.

"So about two weeks later, we all met back up on Melrose Drive, down in San Diego. I had six of my bitches with me, and within the first two days, I had pulled in over six thousand dollars in hoe money, without breaking a sweat. These bitches were turning tricks, burning tricks, and burning candles on both ends of the sticks for Daddy. But it wasn't long before I ran face first into a pimp's worst nightmare."

"And what's that, Pops?" I asked

"Shid, another pimp, nephew. I got knocked for three of my bitches all in one day by this nigga Ice-Cream Slim. Pimp nigga slid his game down on my bitches and they chose. I respected the game and kept right on pimping in true pimp fashion, but then, I got hit with another blow about three days after that, when the pimp nigga Big Whitt served me for my last three bitches I had West of Texas."

"Na'll, Pops, them boyz didn't play you like that, did they?" I asked amazed at how he broke this story down to me.

"Yeeeaaa, nephew, that's just how the game goes. You win some and you lose some—you cop some and you blow some," he admitted as he moved his hands from side to side.

"But the objective of the game is to cop more than you blow, it's just that simple. The day Big Whitt served me for my last three bitches, we were all sitting on the outside of this Dairy Queen and I must admit I was the joke of San Deigo, but I took my on the chin," Pops expressed, as he rubbed his hands together and a smile came across his face.

"But when I got up from the table, I walked straight to the phone booth, picked up the phone, and made that call," Pops added, as he took his hand and made a phone like shape. "Once I got back to the table, the nigga Big Whitt capped on me real tough like, when told me 'Waco Rich,' just step to the side and watch the game from the sideline, baby!" Causing everybody to laugh, because he had my ex-bitch Fay massaging his back. I just smiled and popped my collar, and told that nigga, "All baby, I don't cry over spoiled milk. I must admit you and Ice-Berg Slim did Waco Rich a big favor, because I've been known to dump trash on the side of interstates and highways, I said, as I pointed at the bitch massaging his back, as she frowned knowing I had a trick up my sleeve."

"Yea, that's how you handle that situation," I asked.

"I tipped my hat to 'em and told them boys, ya'll knocked a pimp for his second string hoes, my bench warmers, but watch the way my starting line-up take the field tomorrow. My stable of pitch-hitterz will be here baited up to feed a pimp, because a bitch ain't never made me, I made bitches, played bitches, and traded bitches, so mark my word, because a pimp said that."

"That's what I'm talking about, Pops."

"Nephew, you should have seen the face of San Deigo when my bottom bitch Red turned the corner in my 1972 Delta 88, black-on-black like the nightrider. It was her, Lucky, Angie. V, Tiny, Heather. B, and my almost famous breadwinner Bunny, a real blonde/blue white gal, that pulled tricks in the drop of a dime," Pops emphasized as he wiped the sweat from his forehead.

"I made a statement in '79 down in San Diego, and still to this day, I'm one of the first pimps to ever be logged in the Guinness Book of pimps on records. I mean I had my bitches on every corner. And that's when bunny had knocked Ginger right from under Ice-Berg, and Lucky came in with a bad bitch named Bowleg who was Big Whitt's centerfold. I told all my bitches if they can't knock a breadwinner for Daddy, then don't bring me nothing other than the bread."

"I can dig that, so what happened next, Pops!" I added ampping him up to continue on.

"Shid, I had to serve these niggas and get my cap back on, so I strolled to the corner, packed, and ready to roll out, after about three good weeks on the West Coast, I seen Ice-Berg and Big Whitt together. "Lookout baby, like I said, mark my word Waco Rich did that. I make bitches, break bitches, and I traded in my trash, for the next pimp bottom bitches." And that made Pops just feel his-self, because he must've shook my hand as hard as he could, laughing, and smiling, letting me know that he really cherished that moment in his lifetime.

Just then, I heard my name being called over the loud intercom.

"Chance Hilltop."

"Last call for Chance Hilltop!"

And that made me break the conversation and rush toward the door, hoping this correctional officer don't go to tripping on me, behind nothing.

(Chapter 4)

Acres Homes Texas-44-

"Gulf Bank Hustla"

Two years later (1994)

"How are you doing, Ms. Kim?" I asked as I approached the counter, inside our local neighborhood corner store.

Ms. Kim was a nice petite Japanese lady, who stood approximately four foot eleven inches, and was always smiling in real good spirit. We all began to think she was attracted to young black males, because whenever one of us would be holding a conversation with her, her nipples would harden and perk out through her blouse, right in the middle of the conversation, and she would just smile whenever she caught you looking.

To the Kim family, we gave their store a sign of protection by hanging around throughout the day. In which, they've never been robbed due to the fact, and in return for our protection, I had worked out a deal in my favor, to keep my stash of rocks, inside the store, to prevent from having the HPD roll up and finding a small amount of narcotic on me. It was a sweet bargain, and it worked out just fine. Everybody made money to satisfy the moment. The smokers would cash their checks and buy dope, all in one circular motion, without drawing any heat to either one of us. You could find me hitting licks inside the store, deep in the back when no one was looking.

"Me do good, Cry," she replied, calling me by the name she just gave me; I guess it's because to her cry and tear go together. I never asked, I went along with it. I just smiled as I reached inside my pocket and peeled off a five-dollar bill to pay for my Big Red soda, along with a bag of Hot Fries potato chips, when I noticed this dude behind me, eyeballing my bankroll real hard, causing me to frown up, because he wasn't from around here. And I didn't want this nigga to let my baby face fool 'em, because if he was looking for a quick lick, he was in the wrong place for real. So I pulled up my shirt just enough to expose the butt of my P89 Ruger, sending him a message that said it's blood on my money. And once our eyes met, he got the picture, because he backed up as I made my way toward the door and came to a stop at the pay phone. I had to call Popeye to re-up on my next pack.

"What's up, big boy? Swing by when you get a chance," I spoke into the phone, as he agreed.

As I was walking off, Dough-Boy was riding up on his bike, followed by two of his homeboys (Do-Do and Big Butt); two brothers with some crazy ass nicknames, but hey, that's what the whole hood called 'em, so I did the same. The sight of them three just looked like trouble, and nine times out of ten, they were up to no good. My brother knew how to choose his friends.

"Big Bro," Dough-Boy began, as his bike came to a complete stop right in front of me.

"What's up?"

"Listen to this, I got a lick on the other side of the hood for one hundred dollars, and I told 'em I'll be right back," he added, as I just looked at his ass not believing a word he just said, because he's been trying to persuade me to let him start hustling around the store with us. But I kept declining, because I didn't want Momma to find out and get suspicious about what I've been doing on the low. I haven't been to school in like two weeks as it is, but I've been waking up acting as if I'm going, only to end up posted up behind the store 'or' somewhere deep inside a trap house ducked off in Acres Homes, pushing and peddling my rocks.

To us, Acres Homes was in the same condition as the eastside of Waco. Section 8 apartment complex was the hangout spot, where weed smoke filled the air, drug deals were done in plain view, and it was easy to fit right end if you made yourself seen on a regular basis. And once I started hustling, I thought it would be wise if I gave Dough-Boy money, instead of letting him become a part of this street life.

"Mann, Dough-Boy, I already told you, Na'll."

"Just this one time. I get tired of having to ask you for money, when I can make my own!" he emphasized as we continued to walk.

I had seven rocks left inside a sandwich bag, wrapped around my index finger, tucked away in the palm of my hand. As I debated on letting my younger brother get down with me for his first time, just then Popeye's all-white, tinted-out, four-door Delta 88 turned the corner.

"All right, peep this. I'ma say this one time and one time only. Take these seven rocks, give five of them to whoever you said that want to spend one hundred dollars, and ride your bike by the store and you'll sale those last two, because crack sale itself," I said, as I handed him the sandwich bag. "Now, do you got?"

"Yea, I got it."

"That's good, because I want fifty dollars out of the $140 you're about to make," I replied with a mug on my face, not really wanting to as it is.

"Okay, I got you, Big Bro."

"All right, just take care of your business and we'll meet back up later," I ended as Popeye pulled over, and I got in on the passenger side of the car as we pulled off and headed down the street.

"Young Tear, what's up with you, booyy?" Popeye began.

"Shid, you know me, baby, I'm out here trying to get it."

"I see that my nigga, and that's what's up. What's on your mind this go around?"

"I'm shopping for two zips baby," (meaning ounces) I said, as I reached inside my pocket and counted out my entire life savings, $1,339.

"Two ounces, huu, boy, I see you been taking care of your business out here, dedicated to your grind, bleeding that store," Popeye commented as he smiled and made a left turn on De Priest Street, headed toward Willow Run.

"It is what it is. I got to eat by all means, baby!"

"That's real my nigga. Just keep doing what you're doing, and before you know it, we'll be at the top together, standing side by side," he admitted as he pulled in front of his house and hopped out.

Popeye was a real laid-back type of dude; who has been my connection for the past five to six months. He was one of the first cool dudes I met when we moved to Houston about two years ago. We both attended the same high school, but he was like four years older than me. Stayed right around the corner from me, and plus, he sold weed. So we were destined to meet one day soon. And from there, he put me on, and I done finally started having money. I had to hide it from my momma, because she would trip the fuck out if she found out I was hustling and selling dope.

I just turned sixteen years old, and it felt good not having to ask my momma for anything. At fifteen years old, I tried the route of filling out applications at the surrounding supermarkets, but never came close to being hired, because of my age. So when the law of average came and the opportunity presented itself, I took to Hustling, like a fish take to water. And I was too far gone.

I've been acting as if I'm working for this landscape company, cutting grass and trimming lawns, to keep the cheat off me with my mom. In which, it was like, the thought of me having a job made her that much more proud of me. I had certain smokers call and act as if they needed me to come out and cut their grass. Up until, I had a close call one night, when one muthafucker called after midnight and asked my momma could I come cut their grass. It was good she took it as prank phone call, because I was sweating bullets, thinking she had finally found out.

Just then, Popeye came out his house and got back in the car and handed me three ounces. I eyeballed and picked the two that appeared to be the best ones, and gave back the extra one.

"Na'll, just keep it and pay me later, because them my last three and I ain't trying to hold on to it," he said as we backed out of the driveway, and I handed him one thousand dollars wrapped up in a rubber band. Once we made it to the corner of Winter Bay and W. Gulf Bank, I got dropped off and walked to the house.

*   *   *

"How much you got Dough-Boy?" I asked as I began to close the window blinds in my bedroom. In which since I was the oldest I had my own room, while him and Ry-Ry shared a room. Mines' was a big ass garage that was converted into a giant size bedroom, with a washer and dryer hooked up in it. I had it decked out like a one-bedroom flat—a sofa, recliner, an entertainment system, with a king-size water bed in it. Majority of everything in my room I bought from smokers 'or' shoplifters. In which, it didn't matter once it made into my room, it was considered as mine.

"I got $140 like you said I would!" Dough-Boy admitted as he counted out fifty dollars and handed it to me, while pocketing the rest.

"Hit that light switch for me?" I asked Dough-Boy as the room got pitch dark from closing the blinds.

"It ain't working. You must need a new bulb."

"I just put a new bulb in the shocked about a week ago."

"Well, I don't know it ain't working," Dough-Boy said, as he stood there flipping the switch up and down.

"Check the dining room light," I instructed, as he turned and went into the next room and repeated the same process.

"Mann, the lights cut off," Dough-Boy said from the dining room.

"Cut off," I began. "Momma must didn't pay the bill or something," I said, as I walked straight to my mom's room and knocked on her door, until she gave me the approval to come in.

"What's the matter with you?" I asked, noticing her eyes were all watery and puffy, as if she had been crying.

"What's the matter, huu?" she responded before she continued. "You tell me, what's the damn matter?" she said, as she raised her voice and picked up a letter she had lying on her bed next to her, along with a few other letters.

"Chance, your ass ain't been to school in almost three weeks."

"I have been—" I protested.

"Don't fucking lie to me, these damn folks ain't lying on you," she added as she waved the letter at me.

"Here it is, in black and white, your ass has been expelled for too many unexcused absents, so you tell me what's the matter."

I was stuck, because I never thought about the school district sending a letter to notify my mom about me not attending class. I got caught slipping for real, and I could see the hurt in my momma's eyes.

"Here it is, I work my ass off every damn day to put a roof over ya'll head, to put clothes on ya'll back, and to feed all four of ya'll, all by my damn self, and this is how I get treated in return," she was saying as tears began to run down her face.

"I done spent all my damn money paying the rent, the water bill, and these damn folks done cut my damn lights off, and I can't get nobody to do help me out, because everybody say they're broke, and I got seventeen dollars to my name," she replied, as she vented out her frustration.

To sit here and witness my mom at her lowest point in life was palpable. To me, she was one of the most strong-minded, independent women I knew, who did the best she could to raise us right. And to see her like this made me want to just jump up and run full speed out her room, but I didn't have to, because she put me out.

"Get out," she began, as if she was about to get off her bed.

"Get out, right now. I don't even want to look at you're ass right now!" she screamed in a disgusted rage with an unexplainable expression on her face. I dropped my head and turned around, closing the door behind me. In my heart, I knew I had let her down for first time in my life; I could tell from the look in her eyes.

Linda Kay knew her sons were becoming too much to handle on her own. She had even considered the thought of moving back to Waco, once her lease was up. But she declined and continued to push forward. She knew she had to weather the storm, because struggle came before any success, and that's what kept her motivated.

Later on that night after my mom cooled off, I founded myself standing in front of her door deliberating if I should knock or not, until my hands formed a fist and I knocked, only this time with my mind made up to talk to her.

"Momma," I said, as I walked into her room, in which she was lying across her bed full of clothes.

"Chance, what do you want?" she asked as she turned to face me, propping herself up on one elbow, placing a hand under her chin.

"Here," I replied as I pulled out the three hundred dollars I had in my pocket and tossed it on her bed, as she just looked at me and then at the money.

"That's my savings from cutting grass," I lied, hoping to ease the moment.

"Tear, close that door, and let me tell you something," she began in a low tone of voice.

"Now, I don't know who you think I am, but I do want you to know I wasn't born this morning. And I do know cutting grass ain't where that money came from. That's some kind of smoke screen game you've been playing. For one, Tear, your ass don't have any grass-strained shoes or clothes, so explain that?" she asked knowing damn well he couldn't.

"I do-I just-I-I-I—" I began, but my words wouldn't come out.

"I don't want to hear that shit, Tear. I've been around too long to let you run that bullshit on me like that, but I'ma tell your ass this. I do have a good idea just what you're doing, and if my intuition serves me right, I'ma say this one time and one time only," she added with no trace of emotions in her voice, as she sat up on the bed, and I stood there frozen, not knowing just where she was going with this because she was on point about the grass-stained clothes and I got to change that up.

"Tear, what are your plans for the future?"

The question caught me off guard, but I didn't want her to get all hysterical and out of character like she did earlier.

"Momma, I'ma get it together," I assured her, as she just stared straight through me.

"Chance, I told you before we moved down here that I needed you to be a leader and help me with your brothers and sisters. I know I can't buy ya'll all those designer brand clothes, but I do what I can when I can," she began.

"I'm not getting any help from your daddy, like I used to," she added, as she held up a letter that she had received that day from him.

"And I said that to say this, I know what you've been doing, and if you want to end up in prison like your father, just keep that shit up. Tear, I bet not ever found none of that shit in my house, and if I do, I'm flushing it right down the toilet. I'm not going to jail for you or nobody else. If that's the life you want, then make sure you remember this. No one has ever won in that game without going to prison or getting killed," she finished without breaking her cold stare. I didn't know what to think, because I was too far gone to turn back around now. I still got dope to sell, and it was like I'd just received the approval to hustle (only if I did it a certain way).

I'll never forget that day, because I promised myself that my momma would never have to struggle as long as I was alive and free. Me and Dough-Boy came together and took our game to a whole 'nother level. We formed a team, but he had to stay in school, and he was cool with that. It was money to be made, and we had to go out and get it. I became the man of the house at fifteen years old.

(Chapter 5)

School Days for a Hustla

The first day of school around the United States was always like a fashion show. Almost everybody you came in contact with were decked out in the latest gear. And I must admit after a good summer of bleeding the block, grinding hard, and hustling even harder, me and Dough-Boy was stealing the show and giving the fashion show a run for their money. While the females sported tight-fitted capris, jeans, and shirts that revealed their belly buttons and cleavage. And the dudes rocked the latest Jordans, throwback jerseys, and all the new urban wear. Me, I took mine to a more mature level.

I had just turned sixteen years old, parking a 1992 Chevy Caprice (football style) with the windows slammed with 5 percent tint, sitting on sixteen-inch disc and vogues, with four fifteen-inch kickers beating down the block, bumping a gray tape screwed and chopped.

We stepped out the vehicle fresh to death. I was wrapped in rare form, dressed in Ralph Lauren from head to toe; Polo down with the matching sox, with a pair of low-quarter Polo boots with the buckles; half-karat diamond earrings in both ears, with a forty-inch beaztin and an iced-out cross swinging from my neck.

Dough-Boy was rocking a Houston Oiler: "Warren Moon" throwback jersey, with a white hooded sweater underneath, a fresh pair of all white air force ones, with a thirty-two-inch diamond-cut rope and liberty coin hanging from his neck.

We both smelled like a mixture of weed smoke and Issey Miyake, as we strolled through the hallways of Aldine Senior High School.

"Hey, Dough-Boy!"

"Come Here, Tear."

"Damn, can we ride with ya'll!"

Heads were turning as we spoke and glanced at the new and old faces of the 1995 school year.

"Girl, who is that?"

"Girl, that's Tear and Dough-Boy!"

"Are they brothers."

"I think so."

It's crazy how so much can change within just the matter of ninety days. And how so many people adorned and admired the finer things that the streets' life has bought so many young cats like ourselves. After all, we weren't the only young hustlaz in the school house during these times, because it was a few more, young, money-getting nigga shining too. But we did get our recognition when it came to being a part of the staring line-up for getting real life block money.

But no matter what, a person has to always remember that you're capable of being hated on by someone watching on the sideline. In some cases, haters breathe and live right in the midst of your own inner circle.

The game was designed to definitely hand a player his or her share, because haters come in all shapes and sizes and they travel in liquid form.

However, two years has passed since we've moved to Houston, and it didn't take us long to adjust to our surroundings. We had set the tone and made a statement that said we were demanding our respect by any means. In which, we were known, for the simple fact that we stayed in Acres Homes, but in Acres Homes, we were known as the Waco Boys, because we represented Waco, Texas, to the fullest, regardless of the fact.

Me and Dough-Boy had separate classes and homerooms, and that caused us to maneuver the hallways in different directions talking and mingling with a different variety of females and dudes. Once I made my way into my homeroom class, most of my classmates were already seated, as a high yellow, Lisa Ray look-alike was stationed behind the teachers' desk, calling names, takin' roll.

"You must be Mr. Hilltop."

"Yes, ma'am."

"So glad you could join us. Please find a seat."

I scanned the room looking for a seat available, until I took a seat next to a dude I knew named Lil. D.

"What's up Tear, baby," he said, as we greeted one another by giving dap.

"Shid, I'm chilling, but what's up with you, my nigga," I replied.

"Mr. Hilltop," the teacher called out from her desk, gaining my attention. "I asked you to find a seat, not to disrupt my classroom!" she said as she adjusted her glasses and proceeded to continue.

"Good morning, class."

"Gooood moorrnning," we all said in concert with each other.

"Well, as you all can see, I'm your homeroom teacher, Ms. Upshaw, and we'll meet here first thing every morning. Needless to say, I do realize we have a few new faces this year, and that's just excellent. So I would like for everyone to stand up and introduce yourselves to the class, starting with this roll here," she instructed, as she pointed a finger to a female seated in the front roll.

It finally reached me, as I stood to my feet and all eyes were pointed in my directions, I smiled and greeted everybody.

"What's up with it!"

The class started laughing, but Ms. Upshaw clammed that down real quick.

"Mr. Hilltop, could you introduce yourself in the proper manner."

"Okay," I began, "I'm quite sure you all know I'm Chance Hilltop, better known as Young Tear."

"So what school did you attend last year?" the teacher asked.

"I went here for half the year, but then I graduated and went to Gulf Bank High," I chucked, as certain students in the class stated laughing, knowing I was referring to my neighborhood as Gulf Bank High. Ms Upshaw seemed to had turned a bright red, as a frown crossed her face and told me to take a seat.

"Mr. Hilltop, if you keep this up, I will rest assure you that you'll spend your first day of school inside the principal's office, do I make myself clear?" she warned me as I bushed it off.

"Yeah," I mumbled like I don't give a damn.

For the rest of the class, it seemed like we continued to look in each other's direction. And I know right then that this would be another short year for me. Shid, I only came to school for two things; to make my presence be felt and to find me some new hoes to fuck. And that was easy to me.

Once the bell rang, the hallway was back in full swing. Lockers were being opened and shut. Females were talking loud, and the uppity ones were trying to avoid any run-ins with the ones from the ghettos like Lincoln City, Garden City, Goodson Drive, Greenpoint Townhomes, 'or' Coppertree Apartment Complex. You know the cute faces and fat asses, but ghetto ways. Me, I decided to stay the whole week to get locked in with a few females. Aldine was an open campus, with an hour-long lunch period, where students could leave and come back. In which, that was right up my alley.

As I entered the cafeteria and made my way through the double doors, the first thing I seen was the ass on this female standing in line, waiting to purchase her lunch, wearing a tight-fitting tan and brown Louis Vuitton wrap dress, with a matching purse hanging over her shoulders. And from the way she stood, I could tell she was slightly bowlegged. Once our eyes made contact, I headed in her direction and flashed her a smile, as she did the same, revealing a nice deep dimple inside her right check.

"Excuse me, but I hope you don't mind me intruding in your vicinity," I began as I extended my hand, and she complied.

"For the record, no, I don't, since you ask," she replied.

"So what's your name?"

"Carmal is my real name, but everybody call me Wynter."

"Yeeaa, is that right. I like both of those names. The whole concept fit you to the tee."

"And just what do you mean by that?" she asked

"That means I like what I see, standing right before my eyes, as we speak."

"Boy, quit it!"

"Na'll, but I'm for real and I'm trying to take out to eat right now and get to know more about you, Ms. Wynter."

"Is that right?"

"Yea, that's right. Name the place, and within minutes, our meals could be ready."

"Whatever, Tear," she inquired, using his name to let him know she already knew who he was.

"That's real talk, because believe me if you want to eat one hundred dollar bills, I'm the one that can feed 'em to you."

"Boy, you full of game, ain't you?" she chuckled.

"So I take that as a no."

"I wouldn't call it rejection, but just what did you have in mind?" she asked, not really believing out of all the females inside the school house. She had Tear's full attention asking to take her out to eat, while it seemed like the whole cafeteria was staring at them, needless to say, but she had been hearing about him all morning, as other females gossiped and entertained the thought about who was going to get him first. In which, now it looked like she would be the chosen one.

"Like I said, you name the place and we'll be there in the matter of minutes."

"If I do, I want you to know I have to be back here before lunch is over."

"Don't worry about that I got you. Is it a deal or what?"

"Yea, I guess, we can get us a bite to eat, only if you promise to bring me back before lunch end."

"I told you I got you, but I need you to do one thang for me."

"And what's that," she snapped with a frown on her face.

"Look at you, your mind done went in a whole different direction," I began with a smirk on my face. "But I want you to bring one of your homegirls for my lil brother Dough-Boy."

"Oh!" she replied, feeling a little more relaxed, "Yea, I got a homegirl just for your brother."

"Just make sure she ain't one of those ugly duckling running around here, because my brother's real picky," I said smiling.

"Boy, my homegirl ain't ugly."

"We'll find that out in a minute, he'll be the judge of that."

"Well, I guess we will then."

"Let me go find him, and we'll meet ya'll back at my car. I'm parked out front, so here, take these and give me about five minutes," I finished as I handed her my car keys. And we stepped out of line, and I let her walk in front of me and the sway in her hips made me shake my head, because lil momma was bowlegged with a phat ass that giggled with every step that she took.

The best part about being a dope boy inside the school house was that you had all the action at mixing and mingling with all the top-notch females, when all the broke athlete niggas had to wait on draft day to come, and end up with thug niggas' leftovers.

It didn't take long to find Dough-Boy. Because he was just where I expected him to be, on the three hundred hallway, inside the bathroom, squatted down in his dice shooting stand, hat turned to the back, and I could tell that he was winning, because I could hear him talking shit the moment I walked through the door.

"Big Bro, I'm breaking these niggas!"

"Yea, that's good, but hurry up, we got to bounce, baby." "All right, just let me jump this ten," he stated as he shook the dice in his hand and then released them, as they hit the wall and stop on six to four.

"Point!" the houseman Big Yo called out, and slid the money toward Dough-Boy.

"Come on, Lil Bro, let's ride while all the teachers are out for lunch!"

"Okay, here I come Big Bro, let me fall off first," he added, as he passed Big Yo a one hundred-dollar bill to get faded.

"One hundred dollars the dice shoot," the houseman pronounced around the board.

"The dice hit for fifty dollars," Lil City Gas said riding with Dough-Boy, because he was hot on the dice.

"The dice faded, and that's a bet to you too City Gas!" Wolf said, as he handed the houseman *five* twenty-dollar bills and drop a fifty dollar on top of City Gas's money to cover the bet.

"Money, Good, shot the dice shooter," Big Yo called out, as Dough-Boy shook the dice and snapped his fingers, as the dice were released and slightly grazed DJ, another gamblers foot, and stop on six to five.

"A natural-eleven," the houseman called out and slid Dough-Boy the two-hundred dollar pot.

"Mann, fuck that, the dice hit DJ foot," Wolf screamed.

"You know the rules, point seen money gone," Big Yo replied.

"Fuck that, he got to roll that over," Wolf said in a more real demanding tone of voice. He was really mad because he was losing, and he had lost another $150 on that roll.

"Yea, right, I ain't rolling shit over!" Dough-Boy added, and he was still bent down picking up the rest of his money.

"Nigga, you got me fucked up, you must think I'm some kind of-Wolf began but never got a chance to finish, before Dough-Boy caught him with a stiff upper cuff to the chin, that stood his upper body straight up and then made his knees buckle.

Wolf dropped and landed face first on the floor, as Dough-Boy kicked him and reached inside his pockets, flipping them inside out, and taking the rest of his money; then he turned around and pulled out a small caliber 380 from the small of his back.

"Do anybody else got a problem with the way I'm handling this?" he asked, as everyone shook their heads from side to side.

I stood there blocking the door making sure no one made a move on him, but stunned all at the same time. Raging with anger at how this nigga done turned this into an armed robbery.

"Mann, come on!" I said, as he fixed his self and tucked the gun away. We made our way out the bathroom, only to see Big Yo and City Gas taking the remainin' of Wolf's jewels.

We made it to my car. In which, Carmal and her homegirl were already stationed inside, as I got in on the driver side and told him to hop in the back with lil momma. You could sense the tension in the air, because of the expression I had written on my face. And this nigga over there smiling and laughing like ain't shit happen. That type of shit had me steaming on the inside, as I exited Interstate 45 and made a right on West Mount Houston and 249.

"Let's eat pizza," Carmal managed to say, once she seen Pizza Inn come into our full view.

"That sounds good to me," I said in a nonchalant manner, basically because I was still heated about the altercation we just had moments ago.

"Dough-Boy, you know, you tripped the fuck out?"

"Big Bro, fuck that nigga, you seen how he tried to pop fly out da mouth, so I severed 'em," Dough-Boy growled, still ampped up with his adrenaline pumping.

"Nigga you got to use your fucking head and think, that was some petty ass shit," I fired back, as I pulled into the driveway of Pizza Inn.

The females were in a state of not knowing what the hell we were talking about, but whatever it was; it had something to do with them and some mo boys at school. And it had Tear out of his normal laid-back character.

"Man, fuck that shit, it's done now and we can't change it. So let's chill and talk about that later."

In which, I knew he was right, because he just looked at everything from a different angle, when it came to him being involved in any type of drama. He had that just say "Fuck it mentality, and deal with whatever happen or come with it later." That was just him, always has been.

So to ease the moment, after we all finished eating, I drove home, and we found ourselves parked in our driveway smoking a blunt enjoying each other's company. It didn't take long before the weed took a strong effect on the both of them. Her homegirl was wrapped all under Dough-Boy. I must admit she was cute and petite, with a nice full figure on her. We all decided to go inside the house, where Dough-Boy grabbed his lil mamma and lead her to his room, as me and Carmal headed toward mine.

I could tell she was amazed at how I had my room all decked out, like a one-bedroom flat. I had big life-size poster pictures of me, by myself, one with me and my whole family sitting on the hood of my car, and one with me, Dough-Boy, and Crazy Kev, when we were all young, hugged up.

"Who is that?" she asked pointing at that one in particular.

"Ah, that's me, Dough-Boy and my cousin Crazy Kev, when we were all young."

"Boy, you still look the same," she said, as she looked from the picture and then back toward me.

"So I take that as if I was a handsome young fellow."

"Now, I wouldn't say all that," she replied with a grin before asking, "So where is your cousin?"

"He stay in Waco, but he comes down here every chance he gets," I replied, as I ran my hand through her long wavy hair.

"Ain't that where ya'll from?"

"Yea, Waco, that's the birth place."

"Ain't that the place where that man killed all them federal agents or something?"

"Who? David Koresh?"

"Yea, that's him," she said as she turned around and faced me, and I traced the lining of her chin and licked in rim of her lips. She closed her eyes, and moments later, we found ourselves lying across a king-size waterbed, with her leg wrapped over mine, as I ran my hands along her outer thighs, before I found one of my fingers inside of her wetness. She let a slight moan, as she rocked her hips and brushed her pearl tongue against the palm of my hand. I undid her dress and stood up to take my clothes off. She got completely naked, and the sight of her Carmel complexion, without a mark on it, made my dick get so hard that it started to thrive.

Once back in bed, I laid on my back and pulled her on top of me.

"Baby, I like to be kissed all over before we go at it," I said in a real smooth tone of voice. She didn't hesitate to start kissing and licking until she reached my belly button and felt my hard on pressing up against her breast, and the sight of her pretty face looking up to me made me feel like a Boss.

"Baby, kiss me, don't get shy on me now."

"But I've never done it."

"There's a first time for everything, just close your eyes and imagine me to be a freeze pop ice cream," I instructed, as I pushed her shoulders lower.

"Tear, the only way, I'll do it, is if you promise to be my man and only mine!" she said with a derange look on her face.

"Girl, you're already my girl, but I want you to handle your business and do it like it's something you really want to do and be good at it."

"But I've never done it before."

"Well, that can only mean, you have to take your time and use only your lips, while holding your teeth back and suck me like a lollipop," I explained as she positioned herself on her knees, while holding my piece in her tiny hands, with the tip poking out.

Once she relaxed and opened her mouth, she started by working her way around the tip, but slowly my dick started disappearing inside her mouth and she started making a slipping sound. She finally caught a rhythm, and pulled it out of her mouth and licked the main vain, before asking.

"How does it feel?" while having both hands wrapped around his manhood, loving the effects her head game was having on him, because she has never seen a man curl his toes and grab the sheets all at the same time. So that could only mean, her momma had taught her well, but she couldn't let him know. As she started kissing her way back up his upper body, until their bodies were even with one another, and she positioned herself on top in a squatting stands, reaching out and grabbing his piece, and guiding him into her warm, wetness. She was still tight at first, but after she worked her way down and leaned back, grabbing his ankles for balance support, rolling her hips from side to side and then up and down, exposing a full view to Tear, as his dick was sliding in and out of her, and their rhythm came coincided with one another. Then, he flipped her over and placed a pillow under the small of her back and her legs over his shoulders and committed to pounding until sweat formatted on his head and they both couldn't take it no more, and came at the same time. She wrapped her legs around his waist, pulling him down on top of her, as she shook uncontrollable and broke into a deep silence. All you could hear were their breathing as they lay on side of one another.

"Tear, you better not tell nobody what we did."

"Girl, why would I do something like that?"

"I don't know, but I know how you boys do it."

"See, you got me mixed up with them other niggaz, because whatever we do is our business, so you better not tell nobody!"

"Yea, if you say so, but you better not be lying to me either," she was saying, just as her homegirl busted into my room and seen us lying in bed completely naked.

"Girl, come on, we got to get back to school."

"Here we come, so get out of here bitch!" she said, as they started laughing at one another. And we got up, cleaned ourselves, dressed, and exchanged numbers before we dropped them back off at school.

*　　*　　*

On our way back toward the Hood, my pager started beeping, and when I read the number, I realized it was Popeye getting back at me about the work I had ordered yesterday. In which, he was out of pocket, so he told me he'd be getting back at me today to fill my order. I exited the interstate and made a left on Gulf Bank, en route toward Willow Run, a neighborhood inside Acres Home.

"Dough-Boy, that was Popeye right there, so once we get inside the house, you need go get your half on the pack," I said as we pulled back into our driveway and exited the vehicle. Our mom was still at work and wouldn't be home for about another hour, so the coast was still clear. Even though she knew we were hustling, we still had to give her respect by all means.

"Seventeen hundred dollars? Right?" Dough-Boy asked, making sure we were on the same page about the price of the work.

"Yea," I assured him as I called Popeye back and let him know I was at home, and fifteen minutes later, the deal was made, and we had eight ounces of the butter. And the smokers loved it when we had that butter in circular motion; pure, uncut, and cooked-up cocaine, and that's why I liked fucking with Popeye, because he always kept it real and never tried to run bullshit ass game on a nigga.

He was probably one of the few older niggaz that wanted to help and see a young nigga have something in the game when most older cats try to keep a youngest as their footstool instead of trying to help him progress and move forward. Popeye always severed us straight drop and never tried to push that recon whip on us. And that's what built our clientele and our sales up so high.

We each took an ounce a piece, grabbed a fresh razor bland, a plate, and chopped it up, while taking the other six ounces and placing them inside stash spot, of a broken air-conditioner unit, that was only utilized to fill in a void of a once empty window panel.

Just then, we could hear my mom pulling into the driveway, so we rushed to clean up everything and get shit back in order. After all, we didn't want to hear her mouth about nothing. As I looked out of my window, I noticed two Houston Police Officers pulling up right behind her, blocking our driveway, as she exited her car.

"Mann, the laws outside!" I yelled, as I panicked.

"Here, give me the dope," I added, taking the two sandwich bags full of rocks and hid them with the other six ounces; while all I could hear was my mom's voice inside my head, when she told me not to keep no dope in her house, and if the police ever found anything, I was the one going to jail for it. And those thoughts had me heretic, as we walked into the dine and turned the TV on and down, so we could hear what they were saying.

"Excuse me, are you Ms. Hilltop?" the tall dark skinned officer asked.

"Yes, I am, and how may I help you two officers?" Linda Kay said, not really knowing what the problem was.

"Well, we would like to ask you a few questions pertaining to your sons," the younger, fresh-cut white male replied, who looked to be in his early twenties.

"Now what have they done?" she asked, while placing her briefcase on the hood of her car!

"Well, from a report we received, they were involved in a roberry today at Aldine Sr. High School," the other officer filled in.

In which, I couldn't believe my ears and what I had just heard. But I was sure I heard them right, as I turned around and looked at Dough-Boy; who was looking at me shagging his shoulders. Just then, the front door flew open and my mom barged in, stopping her tracks when she seen us.

"You two have a whole of explaining to do!" she screamed as the two officers came in right behind her, cuffed us up, and placed us inside their patrol car.

"Ms. Hilltop," the black officer began, before he was cut off by Linda Kay's hysterical outburst.

"Just take 'em and call me when ya'll get all this shit figured out!" she growled, as she stared at her two sons in a total dismay as they sat inside the back seat of a HPD patrol car like two criminals.

In route to the nearest juvenile detention center and once they arrived, they were booked in for an aggravated roberry and released back into their mother's custody about five hours later.

In which, that was one of the longest five hours of my life. For one, I was booked in for some shit I didn't do and my brother acted as if, ain't shit done happen. He just don't give a damn; is what I was thinking to myself when I'd glanced in his direction with a frustrated look on my face.

"Big Bro, I'ma fuck that bitch ass nigga up when I see him!"

"Nigga, you need to sit your muthafucking ass down somewhere, and use your fucking head. A nigga can't make no money sitting in this bullshit ass kiddy jail behind some bullshit!" I said as I got up to take piss.

"Mann, that nigga crossed the line; you seen him."

"I don't want to talk about it, it's done now," I was saying, when this fat ass country redneck pulled the cell door open and yelled.

"You two get all your shit, because it's your lucky day, mommy done came and got her two low-life peasants."

"Shid, somebody need to come rescue your minimum-wage making ass," Dough-Boy said as I cracked a smile, and the white officer turned red as fuck.

*   *   *

Our ride home was in complete silence. No one said a word, and the next day was a complete disaster. However, we were both expelled for the remaining of the school year and had been banned from attending all Aldine Independent School District schools. That was enough to make our mom go berserk. She was fed up. And the aftermath of that incident caused her to make the decision to put a two-week notice in to transfer her job and move back to Waco once her lease was up on their house next month.

In which, she knew she needed help with raising her two oldest sons. They were becoming too much to handle without a father figure to monitor their up-bring. And right now, she couldn't take it any more.

She hated that she had to accept the fact that Tear was getting his self involved with drugs at an early age, just like his father. Needless to say, but it was his help that kept her from struggling and living a check to check life. He had took the role of being the man around the house. And he did a damn good job of it. He paid half of all their bills, he purchased food stamps that put extra food on their table, he bought clothes for everybody, and he was doing all this at the mature age of sixteen. But she had enough. She couldn't do it on her own. So she decided that Waco was the best opinion.

All Linda Kay wanted was for her kids to grow up and become somebody in life; without having to take penitentiary chances, but it seems like she was fighting a losing battle and the streets were about to win again.

CHAPTER 6

Home Sweet Home

The Heart of the Streets

The sun was shining, behind a cloud, giving the shy that real deep gloomy look. Wind slightly blowing as we rode through the eastside of Waco—a place that looked as if it has been bombed and left for dead by the city. You have run-down rows of houses, flanked by empty lots, filled with broken glass bottles, milk crates turned upside down, and abandoned under one hundred year oak trees where drug addicts and wine heads hang out together discussing the good old days. Whereas local drug dealers stand on the corners, with guns tucked away in their waistlines, and even bigger guns stashed away under tree bushes, just in case rivals came around and looking for trouble.

Waco is a place where a person's almost destined to become a product of your environment. There's only so many job opportunity, and a few will prefer to hire ex-cons, leaving them to be released with a even more less successful rate of gaining a good-paying job. It has a nice size chicken factory, about a half a mile outside of town that can only hire so many people. Leaving the rest to force feed their selves and let the streets supply 'em with a job.

You have high drug activity signs everywhere, buried knee deep into the ground, as it marked the spot to the place we call home. The corner of 400 Lottie and 1300 Table street. Like the old saying goes, no matter how far you fly away from the nest, a trip home will always snap you back to reality.

At first, I hated the thought of moving back to Waco, after staying in Houston for about full three years. To me, Waco was too small and slow. Houston always had something going on, rather it was a pool party, fish fry, car show, or something; it was always somewhere to go.

But after about a good three months of really being back, I can't lie, it felt good to be back home. The Eastside, is a place like no other, it's broken down into smaller version, with a real live low-scale look to it. Violence was part of the norm, because you had gorillas running with gorillas, snakes sliding with snakes, and it will always be left up to you to decide if you would be the predator or the prey. Because Waco is a town where killers kill killers and jackers jack jackers. And it's normal for a chid to witness a drug dealer become successful in the eye of the public, and then hear about the same drug dealer become a victim in a drug deal gone bad, mean-less to say, but that's life in the streets of any town if there's drugs involved. Not just in the Heart of Texas. The crack epidemic has been taking over and put the game in a headlock. It has given the poor something to live for. And it has been good to us.

As me and Crazy Kev were walking through Richland Mall, in search of buying us a few new outfits for the club tonight, I heard a familiar female voice coming from behind me.

"So you can't speak?" she was saying as she tapped me on my shoulder. And once I turned around, a smile quickly crossed my face, revealing my fresh-polished rack of gold teeth trimmed in invisible set diamonds.

It was Dakota Washington, an old classmate—half Italian and Black female with real light hazel eyes and long jet black wavy hair, wrapped in a ponytail. She still looked the same, since our days of middle school, only looked more like a grown woman. Her body structure had all the right curves and the definition of her hips were obvious, as the jeans she was wearing had a tight grip on 'em. I couldn't help but to observe her from head to toe, as we gave one another a hug and greeted for old times' sake.

"What's with you, girl?" I began as I held her hand before releasing it. "I haven't seen you in a whole minute," I replied still smelling the sweet smell of her White Diamond perfume.

"Na'll, I think it's been a minute since I last seen you," she admitted.

"Shid, I've been around, so you couldn't have been looking too hard," I added as we both smiled.

"Boy, the last I heard about was that you were staying in Houston somewhere."

"I was, but I've been back for about the past three months, and like I said I haven't seen you around, but what's life like for you. I know you're taking care of your business out here."

"Yeeeeaaaa, as of right now, I'm attending MCC, but I've been debating about enrolling at the University of Texas at the beginning of next year first semester."

"Girl, that's good, you make sure you do just that too. So who's the lucky dude in your life, if you don't mind me asking."

"Dude, boy, I'm as single as single can be. I haven't really had the time to do the relationship thang, and plus, I don't have time for the games some dudes feel the need to play."

"I can dig that, but why don't we exchange numbers and pick this conversation back up on over a nice meal at my expense."

"That sound good to me, and I know you better call me too," she was saying, as she unzipped her purse and wrote her number down and took mine; oblige to exchange numbers before we departed and went our separate ways.

*   *   *

"Damn, cuddy, who was that?" Crazy Kev asked, as we entered Foot Locker.

"That was Dakota, one of my old classmates."

"Yea, she's super straight baby," he added, meaning she was right for the picking.

"Don't trip baby, I'ma handle it for the home team," I replied as we gave one another dap. In which, it has always been a gift of gab for us to be approached by nice-looking females, because of the way we carried ourselves. Not to mention, it wasn't a problem for us to see something we liked and be willing to break the silent barrier by introducing ourselves. That's just the way it is, when you believe in yourself and stand firm on it.

After we finished shopping, we found us a table in the food court area and a conversation over chicken sandwiches and fries.

"So Tear what's up with ol' boy from H-Town?" Crazy Kev asked in between bites.

"Shid, I'll find out once we finish up this last batch, because I'm going up there in a few days," I stated, as I took a sip from a Big Red soda.

"Do you think he'll drop the price this time?"

"He said he had a sweeter deal for me, so we'll find out then, but I'm sure he will. If not, then we keep doing what we're doing, pump til' it bleed!" I responded, because everything was running smoothly since we moved back to Waco. We were taking a whole key; breaking it down to the lowest denominator, pushing it rock for rock, going lick for lick, and the money was coming in at a all-time high; to the point where we were able to turn a quarter brick into a three keys purchase in less then two and a half months. The trap house we had on the corner of Lottie and Harrison was moving no less than six ounces a day in all rocks. We refused to sell weight, because it brought too much attention, so we kept it plain and simple. We sold straight, pure, uncut crack cocaine to smokers only. In which, our rocks were so damn humongous that it didn't take long before we had a million-dollar spot. And that shit had me on the Interstate, riding cruise control with bundles of dope tucked away in the stash spot. Needless to say, but that's how I earned the title of being the Interstate Emmitt Smith, from running back and forward and up and down the highway, going from Waco to Houston and then from Houston back to Waco to re-up. To us, it became a system that operated like clockwork. I'd go pick up the work by myself, come back, and then break it down amongst the three of us. Everybody knew the position they had to play, and we played it without a problem. Whenever the forecast predicted it to snow, we all became the block snowman that kept a tight leach on the amount of money we made of every package. In which, the money made us hustle even harder, staying up through the wee-hours of the night and every rock in the pack was gone. And it was normal for one of us to stay up for two or three days with no sleep. In which, the money from the grind made our life worth living, and at times, the streets only bless a person with a cat-nap that automatically amp us up; for another day in the game that was a part of our everyday agenda. And almost everyone we came in contact with live the same lifestyle we lived. But to us, the game made the sunshine everyday, and that's all we knew, and that's all that mattered.

*   *   *

The night was still young, as we all met up and followed one another to the Club DV8. Me and my homeboy Odis were riding together in his pearl white trophy truck; while Dee-Wee and Dough-Boy rode together, as J.B., Chipper and Crazy Kev rode in his car.

Tonight was Cocaine Wayne's big birthday bash, and the hood was doing it real big once again. It seemed like the whole Waco came out to support the cause. However, he was considered to be one of the major player in the underworld. The man behind at least 75 percent of the drugs that enter and sell thoughout the streets of Waco. It was once said that he was plugged in with some real big Mexicans down in the valleys, and that's why it was never a drought, and his supply of work was plentiful.

It was one of those nights where the VIP section was marked off with a thick black velvet rope, that separated the hood ballerz and paper chaserz from the regular crowd.

And once we all exited our cars, we kept it gutta, bypassing the long ass line, walking straight to the bouncer, handed him three hundred dollars and mobbed through the VIP double doors. The club was wall to wall jammed pack, as we threw deuces and got greeted by what seemed to be the whole Waco.

"Heeeyy, Dough-Boy, what's up with you?" this bad ass, little, high yellow bitch said, as we walked toward our already reserved booth by the bar.

"Damn, Me-me, what's with you, I see you still playing your little mind games," Dough-Boy managed to say, as he reached out and pitched her belly button, causing her to giggle.

"It ain't even like that, but I've been busy lately."

"I've heard that one before, but what's up tonight? You don't look that busy to me, or should I ask can you get away or what!"

"If I can, then what?" she asked in a sassy manner.

"You already know it's whatever on my end."

"Well, let me make sure the coast is clear, before I give you a for sure answer."

"Don't make a nigga wait all night!"

"Boy, I'll let you know in about twenty to thirty minutes," Meme said as she hit him on the arm in a girly way, while Dough-Boy stepped back and took another good look at her body; in which, her waist was so small that it made her ass, thighs, and hips look a whole bigger than they actually were.

"Just make sure you do that too," he replied as he turned around and made his way toward the male restroom.

It wasn't long before Tear had spotted Dakota and a few of her friends all chilling close to the booth we were en route to. So we approached their table, in rare form.

"If you all don't mind, I'd like to buy a round of drinks for the lovely lady," I replied, as I made my way toward Dakota and extended my hand, as she did the same.

"Na'll, Tear, I'ma buy hers!" Crazy Kev jumped in pointing at one of her homegirls, who in return started blushing.

"And I'ma buy hers!" Dee-Wee and Chipper announced as they chose her other two friends; as my boy Odis stood there talking to Lil

A and Night-Train. And after the waiter came back with our orders, we all talked and laughed, as me and Dakota was making plans to meet up tomorrow. She glanced over my shoulders and pointed.

"Look!"

Once I looked, I noticed Dough-Boy angering with a nigga that I'd never seen before. And that caused us all to jump up and head in that direction, but before we could get there, the nigga had took a swing at Dough-Boy as he weaved, dipped, and then landed overhand right, that spun the nigga halfway around. Needless to say, but this caught the attention of Big Tyrone and Lil Travis who seen it was Dough-Boy involved in the altercation and jumped right in without hesitation. Eastside niggaz were everywhere, punching and swinging, and mopping anything that wasn't from around our way; just then, shots ranged out inside the club.

Everybody was ducking and running, trying to get out of harms, except Dee-Wee. He was standing in the middle of the club with a fully loaded P89 Ruger pointed toward the roof. Everything was moving too fast, even me, as I made it outside and took a good look around.

"Lookout Tear, over here," my homeboy Odis was saying as he waved one of his hands in the air, with a gun in his other hand, standing behind the open door of his truck.

"Where everybody at?" I asked out of breath, breathing hard.

"Over there," he added pointing toward Crazy Kev's car, as we hopped in and pulled onside of them.

"Mann, follow me," I ordered as they both started their cars, and we all drove and parked in front of my aunt Dee's house.

"Nigga, what the fuck is wrong with you two!" I huffed ready to fire off on the both of these niggas for doing that stupid ass shit. As the both of them just sat there tired, smoking a Newport trying to calm down their nerves.

"Mann, take these niggas home, Crazy Kev. Both of 'em drunk and I'll catch up with ya'll tomorrow," I added, as me and Odis hopped back inside his truck and he dropped me off at home.

(CHAPTER 7)

Three Months Later

Dakota couldn't help but to stare at Tear in amazement as he held the wood grain steering wheel with one hand, while breaking down a bag of weed that was stationed in middle of his lap with the other hand, in which, after seeing him do this on a number of occasion, still made her a little nervous, but she realized that smoking weed was a part of his everyday life, and she made no attempt to try and change it. In fact, that's all he ever did, but not once have he tried to entice her to indulge in getting high with him. However, he preferred a woman who was the complete opposite. And that she was. There was no mistaking; they were officially a couple, enjoying all the lovely things couples do together.

"Baby, grab me a Big Red soda and put twenty dollars on pump five if you don't mind," I began after pulling into a gas station, parking onside of a gas pump, and handing her some money, while I finished rolling up a blunt.

"Okay, is that all you want?" she asked.

"Yeeaa, that's about it, unless you feel like giving me my kiss right now," I added, as I reached out and rubbed her chin.

"I'll pass on that one," she said with a smile on her face, as we both stepped out the car, laughing at one another. It wasn't long before, we were back en route toward our destination.

"Dakota, play that Mary J. Blige CD."

"Where is it?"

"It should be in the back of da folder," I replied, as I reached for my blunt and fired it up.

"Okay, here it goes. OOOOHHHH, you need to stop smoking!" she said as she turned her nose up once the smell filled the air, and she cracked the window.

"Girl, don't start that tripping again."

"I ain't tripping either. You know I don't like the smell of that stuff!" she added as she turned to face the window. "And you still haven't answered my question."

"And what's that?"

"About the movies, are we going or not."

"Girl, I already told you we were. What time do the movie begin anyway?"

"At seven thirty."

"Oh, we still got enough time to get us something to wear, and then head back to my place, take a shower and get dressed," I responded, as I patted her leg. It was something about being in his presence, that made her feel secured. He knew how to touch her in ways that she has never been touched in. He always gave her his undivided attention, despite the fact that he smoked weed and of what everybody else had to say negative about him being with other females, but when they were together, to him, it seemed that nothing else really mattered. He was the same dude every day and not once did he switch up his character. He would buy her things spontaneously and shower her with designer name clothes and shoes for gifts. And that something no man has ever done or thought about doing for her, whereas other dudes only seemed to be out for just one thing. But Tear was different; always cool, clam, and collective.

Standing in at six feet three inches and 205 pounds, his frame toweled over her five foot two inches, but that's the way she preferred her man; tall, dark, and handsome.

"Come on, baby, let us find you something to model in for me tonight. I said, as I reached out and grabbed Dakota's hand and pulled her closer to me, as we entered the lovely Victoria's Secret. She was blushing the whole while, because she had never been shopping for lingerie with a dude before, so this was something new to her and it felt sexy. In which, that's what she loved the most about being with him, because it was no shame in his game.

"How may I help the lovely couple today?" a nice-looking, middle-aged white female sales rep asked us upon our arrival.

"Oh, how are doing, we're just looking around at this moment, but it would be our honor to ask for your assistance if we have any," Dakota replied in a real professional manner. In which, we bought a few sexy pieces and had a few laughs, as we thanked the sales rep and made our way to exit the store en route to have her nails done.

"Hey, girl, what are you two doing?" Dakota asked as she acknowledged Meme and Tamikco as they all greeted one another, with a hug.

"Girl, we're just doing what we do best," (shopping) they said in unison, with a giggle.

"Girl, me too."

"Oh, we see that!" Meme replied as they all chuckled referring to Dakota's bag of lingerie.

"Girl, I see you're still crazy and ain't changed a bit," Dakota was saying to Meme, as she softly hit her on the shoulder.

"Hey, Tear, what's up with you?" Meme asked, as she turned attention toward me.

"I'm chilling, you know me, staying all the way low key," I said as I folded my arms.

"Where's Dough-Boy?" she asked.

"I haven't seen him today, but he's probably on the Eastside somewhere," I replied as I noticed her other homegirl giving me that eye. They all continued to talk a few more minutes, before we all went our separate ways.

"I seen the way ol' girl was looking at you, as me and Meme were talking," Dakota began once we were out of their earshot.

"Then, you have said something and checked her ass," I replied as I pitched her on her ass, turning her statement into a joke, causing us both to enjoy the moment of laughter. After she got her nails done, we went back to my place to freshen up and headed out to the movies an' seen "*Set it off*" with Jada Pinkett and Queen Latifah staring in it. Afterward, we sat in Basket & Robbin, shared a jumbo banana split, and discussed our plans for the future, before I decided to take her home because it was getting too late and I knew she had an early class tomorrow.

"Well, I hope you enjoyed yourself tonight," I said, as we reached her porch and I placed her hand in mine.

"Believe me, I did," she replied as we faced one another.

"Make sure you call me once you're released from your noun class or whenever you find time."

"I will, you just make sure you stay out trouble," she added, as she turned to unlock the front door, before turning back around. "Be careful, Tear, is all I'm saying," she said as she leaned in, and we found ourselves in a warm embrace that seemed to block out everything that existed, as I allowed my tongue to lick the lining of her lip, before I finished with a peck to seal the moment. It's like the sun would shine every time we were together, because nothing else really mattered. Once our lips broke the kiss, Dakota looked at me through watery eyes.

"Good night, Tear. I'll call once I get out of class."

"I will be waiting, and I'ma hold you to that," I said with a smile engraved on my face, as I hopped back behind the wheel of my SS Impala and smashed out.

(CHAPTER **8**)

Fresh Off Lock

Black Ty-*Suited up for the Field-*

"Where that boy at?" Crazy Kev said as he walked into his mom's house, looking for Black Ty; who had just came home from doing four and a half years in TDC (Texas Department of Correction) for an armed roberry that him and Crazy Kev had committed, but he had served the time, because his fingerprints were the only ones traced back to the scene of the crime; from a can soda that he had dropped, that linked him to the crime, and plus, he was pointed out in a lineup by the victims; in which, he stuck to the G-Code and kept it gangster. I didn't take a deal to get a lighter sentence, like most niggas are doing now-a-days. He took his on the chin, snitching wasn't in his blood. They were all family; not by blood, but by the love that had for one another. When everybody else gave up on him, the Hilltop family always was there for him, with arms wide open. Shid, he was considered a Hilltop, his name was always enlisted in the family tree of every family reunion. So this was his family; always have been and always will be.

"What's up, baby!" Crazy Kev said as soon as he walked into the living room and seen Black Ty.

"What's up, my nigga!" Black Ty replied with a big ass smile written on his face, and that fresh off-lock glow to it, as they hugged one another and started to play boxing like old times.

"Nigga, let me see that shit," Crazy Kev said smiling, as they hugged one another again.

"Damn, my nigga, it's been a long ass time."

"Shid, you think I don't know."

"Hell, yea. I see your ass been down there on them weights. Done got your swolle on and shit."

"I had to do something to pass that slow ass time."

"I can dig that, but come on, let's ride and get your ass back together and stop all that muthafucking smiling friendly ass nigga."

"Nigga, fuck you," Black Ty said as the both laughed and headed out to Crazy Kev's car.

"Here, put this in your pocket," Crazy Kev said as he tossed a wod of cash, wrapped in a rubber band into Black Ty's lap and began to back out of the driveway.

"It's all one hundred dollar bills, baby. Our petty stealing days are over, ya dig. It's real money out here in these streets, but don't trip my nigga, just take your time, and once you feel like you're ready, 'the world is yours for the taken,'" Crazy Kev emphasized in his best scarface impersonation.

"What's been going on out here, since I've ben gone?" Black Ty asked as he rewrapped and placed the five thousand dollars back in its original rubber band and stuck it deep down in the front pocket of his institutional release, tight-fitting, 501's Levi jeans.

"Shid, my nigga, these blocks been treating a nigga swell out here. You know ever since Tear and Dough-Boy moved back from Houston, the game been lovely without a doubt."

"I see," Black Ty replied as he took a look out the window and smiled to himself, as Crazy Kev continued to go on about how things done changed since he been gone.

"And you know Tear, he got a plug in the city, and that's what keep a nigga afloat; even in the middle of a drought." "That's what's up, but what's up with the plex?" he asked trying to see who was considered an outsider to their inner circle."

"Mann, everybody getting money right now. The Eastside ain't beefing with nobody like we use to. Everybody trying to get this money out here right now," Crazy Kev added as he pulled in front of a house that was wrapped in burglar bars from the front to the back.

Come on, let's run in here, right quick. I got somebody I wanted you to see.

"Who shit is that?" he asked as they both walked past this black-on-black 1996 SS Impala sitting on twenty-inch blades and vogues.

"You'll see nigga, so stop all that muthafucking smile," he added as he started rambling with the burglar bars trying to find the right key that fit.

*   *   *

"Mann, let me show you how to do this shit. I know how much baking soda to put on every package," Dough-Boy said as he stood over the stove, experimenting with an ounce of powder, as I stood over his shoulders and watched his every move. He had the Pyrex in one hand, holding it in the air under the light, with what seemed to be a gel-like substance formatting and falling to the bottom of the jar. The sound of someone rambling with the front door made us both stop in the mid pause.

"Who the fuck is that?" we both said in a whisper conjunction as we looked at one another. Someone had opened the side door, but the dead bolt lock prevented it from opening. I reached for my smoke gray Mac 90 off the table and flipped the safety button off.

"Who is it?" I yelled as I inched closer toward the door, hoping like hell this isn't the FEDs.

"Cuddy, open the damn door, nigga." Crazy Kev's voice brought a sign of relief to the both of our faces. Dough-Boy was ready to dump the work inside a bucket of acid, which we kept underneath the kitchen sink, just in case. And I was ready to unload and empty the whole clip.

"Nigga, your ass know to call before you come," I began as I unlocked the dead bolt lock and seen my young nigga Black Ty.

"What's up, baby?" I said with excitement in my voice, as I sat the Mac 90 back down and we embraced one another.

"Glad to see you, finally, made it back home. Shid, we been waiting on your muthafucking ass, for real."

"Shid, I'm glad to be back out here my damn self." Black Ty said as he stood there smiling and grinning from ear to ear. He had finally made parole, and now, he was back in the midst of his family. Niggas that was like his brothers, the ones that kept it real with him the whole five years he was in TDC. He didn't have to want for much, not when it came to money and pictures. He was content with the way they all showed him love. Crazy Kev had started fucking a unit manager, who worked at the same facility he was housed at. And you know the power of some grade A dick and a little money here and there, can make a bitch jeopardize her entire life savings, not saying that it wasn't worth it, because she would smuggle him cases of tobacco, weed, and anything that consist of contraband; everything except some pussy. She was stuck on Crazy Kev, but she did turn him on to one of her other homegirls who just loved to watch him jack off at nighttime after rack-up. She would sometimes let him stay out late night to clean up the whole dorm, while all the other inmates were either sleeping or zoned out in their own little world. And on those nights, she would entertain him with oral pleasure. In which, he did his time with a smile written on his face, on the count of these boys.

"Look out bitch," Dough-Boy said as he strolled into the room smiling again.

"What's up, hoe?" Black Ty shot back, as we all cracked up like old times again.

"Nigga, I told you boys I'ma make this dope lock up like a science project," Dough-Boy added as he held the Pyrex up in the air at eye level, twirling it around for us to examine the cookie that formed at the bottom.

"Ty, this nigga want to be Betty Crocker so muthafucking bad, that he have dreams about cooking up dope," Crazy Kev replied, pointing at Dough-Boy as water dripped from the Pyrex jar.

"Mann, let's go fade the mall and get this nigga out of these tight ass 501 jeans."

"Nigga, fuck you."

*   *   *

The day was still young, and after we made our rounds through Richland Mall and did all the shopping we could do, we went to this local college bar, Bronco Billys, a restaurant within the University of Baylor parameter. Students just looked at us as we enjoyed ourselves like we were all kids again. After we ate, we all went to the Playa's Ball to watch a few strippers slide down a few poles. The sound of 5th Ward Boyz was bumping through the speakers, "Pussy, Weed, and Alcohol," while three strippers were all on stage dancing with one another as the DJ's voice came blurring through the air.

"I see the fam' done walk through the door," causing heads to turn, then the DJ added, "Fresh meat! Young Black Ty fresh off lock, and it's good to have you back, baby boy." Everybody was showing him love, and the DJ jammed that Lil KeKe, "balling in the mix." Niggas were bobbing their heads as strippers pranced around. We pulled up to the bar, ordered our drinks, and gave a toast.

"On three, nigga, it's 'We All We Got,'" Dough-Boy said as he did the countdown.

"One-two-three. 'We All We Got,'" as we all started laughing and enjoying the rest of the night.

(CHAPTER 9)

POLO

—Playas Only Live Once—

I put on a pair of black dress slacks with a white and black pinstripe Ralph Lauren sweater, and then slipped my foot in a pair of Kenneth Coles. For my first time, I laid eyes on her at the mall. Lil mama was bad! So you know, after doing a background check, opportunity presented itself, and I was all for the taking.

While pumping gas at this convenience store, I heard my name being called with a soft feminine exclamation. Once I turned around, I seen T'meikco behind the wheel of a navy-blue Honda Accord, as she stepped out in a pair of painted-on jeans with an icy white halter top, Chanel sandals, and Chanel shades covering up her eyes. "Let me find out, you were going to ignore me," she began.

"Why would I do such a thing," I said with a smile on my face, causing the sun to shine down on my gold's, as I finished pumping my gas and placing the pump back in its slot, because the last time I seen you, I spoke, but you paid me no mind. I guess it was because you were with your girl."

"Now, you know how that shit go, it was no disrespect toward you, bad timing I guess," I began as we entered the store.

"So what brings you out this way," I asked.

"You never know," she added with a smirk on her face, as she stepped in front of me and I could watch her ass move as she made her way to the freezer and bent over to get a pint of Blue Bell strawberry ice cream.

"Make that two of 'em," I said causing her to bend back over, showing the rim of her black G-string.

"What kind?" she asked looking over her shoulders seeing that I had my eyes glued on her ass. Ass was phat, couldn't help but to look.

"Boy, what kind do you want"

"Shid, you-I mean, whatever kind you got."

"Get your mind out the gutta."

"It's hard sometime, especially when I found myself distracted."

We both laughed because she looked down and seen the rim of her G-string herself.

After paying for our items, we both walked back toward our cars.

"So when can I get your number," I asked as we made eye contact with one another.

"It just depends," she replied.

"Depend on what?"

"It depend on if you can keep it between me and you and me and you only."

"Shid, I know how to play my position, can you?"

"Tear, I'm for real. Don't play no games with me."

"I got you cutie, so take that frown off your face," I said, as we exchanged numbers, and weeks later, we were on our way to our first date.

* * *

T'miekco Michigan, the daughter of a African American navy seal commander, who blessed me with the opportunity to witness the sight of five feet four inches 135 lbs, hazel eyes, and bowlegged cocoa butter caramel skin complexion, without a mark, scar, or scratch on her body. Her mother was of Philippians' and Samoan decent, and her slanted eyes and long ass, and shoulder-length wavy hair gave her that foreign exotic appearance. Small breath, but a super small waist with a walk stiffed her hips and stands that locked her knees and made her body structure seem even more bowlegged than she was. So it was a must that I overlooked the fact that she was the wife of a nigga that had more money or more dope than me. Shid, he wasn't part of my team, so it was fuck 'em as far as I was concerned. I've only been back in Waco for nine months, and I don't fuck with trash bitches. I fuck with *bad bitches*. That was my motto. Houston had installed standards in me when I came to my ideal women. But T'meikco was already taken, so entertainment only was the category I placed her in. Plus, I was satisfied with the one that I had at home. But you know how it is when you grow up in a world where your mamma tell you, "You better not tell your daddy," and your daddy tell you, "You betta not tell ya mamma." And that leave you to grow up and become a playa that live that same repetitive cycle. I picked up my cellular phone and dialed her number and waited until I heard her answer.

"Hello!"

"May I speak with T'meikco?"

This is she. Can I ask who speaking, she commented already knowing.

"It's Tear. I was calling to let you know I'll be there in about twenty minutes."

"All right, I'll be parked on the same side as Dillards," she added letting me know where to find her once I reached our approved destination.

"Bet that," I replied as I flipped the off button on my phone and tossed it on the bed, next to my wallet and keys. Put on my jewels and sprayed some Chrome Azzaro on to add the finishing touch, as I checked myself out in my seven-foot inch full-length wall mirror and thought to myself,

"A Real Playa Only Live Once, a that I am!"

As I gathered my things off the bed and headed toward the front door, a smile somehow became engraved on my face. However, this was my first date with T'meikco aka a woman of true meaning.

(CHAPTER 10)

The First of the Month

It wasn't long before Black Ty found his-self suited up and ready to hit the block full speed like a rookie running back, coming straight out of high school. Him and Crazy Kev were posted up on the corner of Edge Way and Clifton Street curb serving. Dough-Boy paced back and forward from the stove to the sink, trying to get the cocaine to transfer into crack rock form. It was one of those nights on the block, where smokers were coming from everywhere. Cars were pulling up, back to back, as smokers got out, went around the house, got served, and drove off. Lookouts were on every corner, ready to give them the heads up if the police were anywhere in the vicinity. Barrels of acids were in place just in case they had to operation as in full swing, and this was everyday life in the hood.

"Lil Archie Lee," a female voice called out from behind them, causing them both to turn at the same time, only to see that it was Sonja, the school teacher, coming toward them, calling Crazy Kev by his father's name. Sonja the school teacher has been around the hood for years. She was once the prettiest woman we ever laid eyes on. She was the local elementary fifth grade teacher that we all had, but she failed the test and has been down along dark journey ever since in the game. Through it all, she still tried to strut in a pair of rundown banana yellow high heels. She was dressed in a faded, colorful sundress that she has worn one too many times. School teacher; let the streets steal her beauty from her. Her once blemished free face is the complete opposite now that the streets have won. It's a pale yellow with blackheads and holes, all in it; the signs of real hard life. She's reminded every day of what she used to be, because everybody called her school teacher.

She made it closer, stopped in front of them, and asked in a sweet tone of voice, "Are you holding, baby?"

"What's up, school teacher," Crazy Kev asked as he just observed her from head to toe.

"Baby, I need a wakeup to get myself started for the day."

Crazy Kev and Black Ty started laughing because dope fiends always came up with some shit to get a hit.

"Mann, its past eleven o'clock at night, and plus, you still owe me seven dollars from the last time."

"I know, baby, but let me get it together, and I'll make it up real soon. I promise," she said in a wining voice.

"School teacher, we ain't gonna keep going through this shit," Crazy Kev said as he reached inside his sandwich bag and picked out a twenty-dollar rock and handed it to her.

Most drug dealers around the way saw and treated crackheads as if they were less than human being, but not us. We gave each individual a fifty dollar monthly credit line. So they had to use it wisely. This was our everyday life and we were a part of the underworld that society considers as being dysfunctional. We have witnessed the streets swallow family members whole, succumbing from one pitfall to the other, face-to-face with rock bottom, but can't comprehend the harsh reality of their situations. We understood the underworld better than anyone, who has never been backstage at a crack epidemic concert. Our intentions was to never kick you when you down on your luck. That was our way to motivate you to go out and get it. Everyone was satisfied with the outcome of the game plan because a good crackhead could be more valuable to you than a member of your own team. You just have to know how and when to make use for 'em.

"Your ass owes me twenty-seven dollars now!"

I know, baby, I really appreciate this, and I'll be back to take care of you sometime tonight," she added as she turned and disappeared into the darkness of street life, in real true crackhead form, as Crazy Kev walked into the house, leaving Black Ty outside to hit licks.

Dough-Boy walked over to the kitchen table with water dripping from the cookie he had clapped between two tongs and sat it down on a paper towel, in front of a small fan that was stained on the table to dry up the crack faster. He had finally learned how to bake bricks, like Betty Crocker, and at times, he'd be in the kitchen from sun up to sun down, standing on his feet, working three to four Pyrex's all at one time, bringing it all back, fork in one hand, in circular motion, working his wrist.

The cook of the click is what we all called him.

"I whipped up that butter baby," Dough-Boy said with a cigarette hanging out the side of his mouth, as Crazy Kev walked in the kitchen.

"Cuddy, I'ma be back. I got too much money on me, so I'ma go put it up. Do you need anything when I come back."

"All right," Crazy Kev replied as he exited the house, got behind the wheel of his car and drove off . . .

It was a little past six o'clock in the evening as we all sat outside of our uncle's gambling shack, just hanging out. It was me, Dough-Boy, Ko-jack, Black Ty, and Lil Dee-Wee sitting on the porch in chairs, with a few old school playas that aren't active in the game no mo'e, mostly retired from the streets, but loved to watch us play the game that they knew so well. I was having a real deep discussion with these two old playas named Frank None and Willie Weights, but silence fell the moment I stopped in mid-sentence, and this navy blue Lexus 430 came to a complete stop right in front of the gambling shack. All four windows were tinted, so no one could see who the driver of the vehicle was.

"Son, who is that," the old playa whispered as he sat up giving the observation his full attention. Both Dough-Boy and Dee-Wee's hands reached toward their waistband, inching closer to their pistols.

Me, myself, I reached under the cushion of the chair I was sitting in and removed my short-nose 357 Smith and Weston. That's when the passenger side door opened and the sight of Meme stepping out in a pair of blue jean Capri brought a sign of relief to all our faces. But when T'meikco rolled down her window, our eyes locked on contact, as I made my way toward the car and took a seat on the passenger side.

Here, we've been doing a whole lot of creeping lately. However, she was a real woman who could hold a nice intolerant conversation. She was more of the homegirl type that made you enjoy her company with ease. That was something I didn't get from a lot of females. So I didn't mind jeopardizing my relationship with her. To me, she was well worth it.

"So this is where you been hiding at," T'meikco asked as I got in on her passenger side bypassing Meme who was en route toward Dough-Boy.

"You know me, hiding ain't my thang," I responded with a smile on my face.

"I can't tell, you haven't returned any of my call."

"That's my bad, but I've been trying to get a lot of things in order, for these past four days, so that's why I wasn't able to get right back at you."

"You could have at less called and said that. That way, I would've known, instead of just leaving me to contemplate on thought."

"Like I said, that's my bad, I wasn't thinking, but I'll make sure I follow your lead the next time," I said as I reached over and rubbed her soft thighs.

"So when will you make room for me," I added as I pinched her.

"Who said I wanted to make room for you, after you did me like this," she teased.

"I did, because you know you can't breathe without me if that's the cause."

"I can value to that, so answer my question when can I breathe again—I mean see you again," I asked as we both started laughing.

"I'll call you tonight and let you know what hotel I'll be in, so be expecting a call, Okay"

"Shid, you got the number, so make sure you do that, and I'll bring *Scarface* the movie for us to watch," I replied as I took the initiative and grabbed the side of her face and pulled her lips to mine, as Meme knocked on the window interrupting us.

"Make sure you call me," I said as I opened the door and stepped out.

"I will. Just make sure you answer your phone when I do."

"What's up, girl?" I said to Meme as I exited the vehicle.

"Hey, Tear," she replied as we exchanged acknowledgement. She shut the door and rolled down the window partially.

"Oh, and by the way, it ain't safe to pull up like ya'll did, because the wrong move would've had this Lexus looking like Swiss cheese," I began.

"Boy, ya'll better be careful," T'meikco added.

"Don't trip. We straight on this end, but ya'll take it easy and you Ms. T'meikco, don't forget," I finished as I tapped the roof of the car. T'meikco winked and pulled off into traffic as we watched the taillights disappear down Hillsboro Drive.

"Man, ain't that Lil Cocaine Wayne Girl," Black Ty asked as I strolled back toward the porch.

"Yeah, that's his first string quarterback, but she's ready to be traded to an all-star team," I said with a smirk on my face, as we all started laughing, and I sat back on the porch with the old playas.

"Young tear, boy, you remind me so much of myself when I was your age."

"Yea, but it'll take me years before I'll be able to walk in your shoes, but I can see myself being just like you when I get your age." My statement caused him to chuckle.

"Younger, I like the way you put that, but to reach my age, it takes years and understanding. You know the game ain't the same no mo. The playas done changed the whole format, and misery love company. One mistake could cause you to lose more than you could ever imagine," he said as he patted my knee. "Just think about this. Like a boxer in the boxer ring, one mistake could lead to a knockout, or in the streets, your life. So youngster, always remember this, always use your head, put all your moves together in your mind, before you react and take it to these streets. Son, play the game like a game of chess, and you'll one day live to be my age. Then, one day, you'll be able to lace up the ones that'll come behind you," pld playa said, as he got up, patted me on the back, and shook my hand before he walked off the porch. The sight of his hands and the roughness of his skin, you could tell he has been around a block or two. And if his hands could tell the story about just who he was, I'm sure they would be breathing taken and unforgettable moments replayed in amazement.

"Youngster, you all take it easy," Willie Weight said as he reached his truck.

"All right," we all said in chorus of one another, as he stopped and turned around and called out my name.

"Chance, I want you to one day read Matt. 26:17-25 whenever you find time," he added as he saluted us like he was still in the army of some sort.

(CHAPTER 11)

For Ever My Sister . . .

"Girl, you know you wrong for that," Meme said as they were pulling off and Tear was walking back toward the gambling shack.

"Bitch, that nigga got it going on, and plus, him and Cocaine Wayne don't fuck around."

"So in other words, what Cocaine Wayne doesn't know won't hurt him," Meme added as they both giggled.

"Have you let him hit it yet," Meme asked slyly while T'Meikco didn't answer, she just gave her a look.

"Bitch, I know you got a thang for that nigga, from the first time you seen him at the mall," Meme teased.

"Girl, he's all right, but you know he got a girl and I got Cocaine Wayne, so we can only go so far," she added.

"T'Meikco, bitch miss me with that shit! You gonna let him hit it, so stop faking."

"I might done let him hit already," she said smiling.

"Yeah, whatever! You would've told me about it, especially if he hit it, right?"

"Girl, your ass crazy," T'meikco added as they headed down Waco Drive en route to Hewitt.

"So have you thought about what Cocaine Wayne would say if he found out," Meme asked, becoming more serious.

"Girl, I ain't worried about him," T'meikco said, as she cut her eyes at Meme, "I'm tired of his shit anyway, all his ass does is give me money, buy me shit, and don't spend time with me, and plus, I'm tired of all his damn lies."

"Wow, where did all that come from," Meme asked knowing her best friend was head over hills in love with Cocaine Wayne.

"Meme, I don't need you to give me another lecture. I'm just playing the field with Tear. In which, he's a cool dude, and I doubt that he'll expose our relationship to anyone in Cocaine Wayne's click, so things are straight on our end," she added, as they continued to ride in silence for the remainder of their trip.

Sometime Meme could get on her nerves, but she was only being herself. They have been best friends since Cedar Ridge Elementary, and over the years, they grew to becoming inseparable sisters that neither one ever had.

They shared so many similarities together. They were both true Leos by birth, born two days apart, in the same hospital. And not to mention they both even experienced their menstrual cycle at the same time and neither one knew what to do. To them, they were sisters who were meant to be part of one another. Not only did their family accept them as sisters, but everyone really thought that they both shared the same mother and father. Because it was always like, whenever you seen one, you seen the other. Hackle and Jackal was their nickname, and still to this day, everyone still refer to them as just that, and they still sit back and laugh at the old time; such as when Meme pissed in the bed, and then poured some water on T'meikco side and made her believe she pissed too; in which, they both received a whipping for it. They were sisters, and the world seems them as being one of the same.

*   *   *

CHAPTER 12

The Coldest Winter Ever

Below Zero in the Heart of Texas

Over the past few weeks, the temperature has started to change dramatically. Daylight saving time has swung into full effect. The nights were now considered to be longer and the days were appearing to vanish right before your naked eye. Leather jackets, sweater, long sleeves, and big boomers were starting to be seen on a daily basis.

It was the winter of 1996, and it was reported to be one of the coldest winters ever in Central Texas's history. But to a real certified hustla, it was the winter he or she loved the best. However, you could save and stack more money in the winter, better you could in the summer; in which, not everyone can stand the change of weather. You have to have that drive to go out and get it, that Hustla mentality, by any means necessary; through rain, sleet, and snow. And that's what separates a real hustla from the average, poor hustla. You know the new outfit and tennis shoe; and he's content type of hustla. And yes, you do see one every dame day, just think about it.

Me, right now, I'm dressed in an all black one-piece installation suit, with a thick hoody on underneath, posted up on a small recliner sofa playing the play station, and smoking a blunt by myself, going rock for rock out the trap houses on Lottie, just as Black Ty walked in blowing and rubbing his hands together.

"Nigga, where in the fuck you been at?" I asked.

"At Sonja, cold ass house posted up."

"Let me find out your ass been down there getting your dick sucked by that crackhead bitch," I said as I hit the blunt and passed it to him, almost choking with laughter.

"You got me fucked up, nigga, that's your job. You know, she always talking about how sweet you meat is, bullshit ass nigga," Black Ty added as he took a stand in front of the floor-mounted electric heater, trying to warm up. He was dressed in the same kind of installation suit that I had on, but his was gray and he had on a red hooded sweater on underneath it.

"It's cold as fuck out there!" he yelled out to no one in particular."

"I know, nigga. The news reporter said that it was thirty-eight degrees outside, so you need to sit your ass down somewhere."

"Nigga, fuck you, you're muthafucking ass, stay on the go."

"I know, and I'm about to go right after I finish up the rest of this pack I got left."

"See, that's what I am talking about, in a rush to go fuck something."

"Nigga, not just anybody, but this a bad bitch."

"Yea-Yea-Yea, heard it all before."

"All right, I don't have to lie to you, you'll see for yourself."

"Who is she then, because I might done fucked her already?"

"I doubt it, your game ain't strong enough, you be fucking too many hood bitches, using that same rundown ass game you got."

"So who is she then, since you done graded this bitch and placed her to be one of the American's next top models."

"T'Meikco, nigga, Lil Cocaine Wayne Bitch!" I emphasized, and he begun to shake his head in agreement.

"Oh yea, now that's a bad bitch, so I'ma give it to you, but in other words, you might be lying on your dick."

"Nigga, you got life and bullshit mixed up, because I'sssa playa and I'sssa never lie on my dick."

"Yea-Yea, nigga, tell me anything, I know how nigga get when it comes to a bad bitch."

"Yea, niggas like you, but not me, baby," I added, already knowing T'Meikco was a top-of-the-line type of female, who not just any nigga can actually say they've even had a moment of her time. Shid, a lot of these nigga are intimidated by a nice=-looking, independent woman, such as herself, but not me, because over the past few months we've been indulging in real open-minded conversation, getting to know more about one another founding ourselves chatting on the phone for hours at times. She really had a head on her shoulders, with a sense of direction and a drive to go out and get whatever it is that she aimed to have in life. She was always on point, regardless of the fact that the guy she was dating was behind over 60 percent of the dope that hit the streets of Waco. But fuck 'em was the frame of mind I was in when it came to him. Because he wasn't the man sitting at the top of the throne of me and my peoples, and what he ate don't make us shit. So his bitch was open game to me. He wasn't a threat to me or my family and that was the way I looked at it. I kept her under my umbrella, and tonight, we had plans to meet undetected, without anyone seeing us out in public. Cocaine Wayne has been in Houston for the past two days, and she wasn't expecting him to be back until late tomorrow night. And plus her best friend MeMe was at home, sick with the flu, and she didn't want to be bothered; so that us all the room we needed to enjoy one another's company.

"Lookout, Black Ty, baby," I yelled out from the living room.

"Yea."

"I'm 'bout to rolled out and head to the Hotel of Hilton"

"All right, just make sure you take care of that other business before you go," he replied as he walked back into the living room.

"That's done already, and Crazy Kev made sure that your end was well put up too. So you know how to get at me if you need anything else," I added as I stood up and placed my fitted cap on my head and put my jacket on.

"Shid, Tear, I'ma make a run later on tonight, and serve these niggaz out of Killeen."

"Nigga, I already told yo ass, but you just won't listen."

"But my nigga, these niggaz paying $7,200 for a short nine-pack (nine ounces), so know I got to get it while the getting is good, and plus these are niggaz I was locked up within TDC, so I know I'm dealing with some through ass niggaz."

"Is that right?"

"Hell, yea."

"Well, just make sure, you watch them niggaz, because nowadays niggaz will try almost anything to get from under the gun!"

"I got it, cuddy."

"Just in case, da Mac 11 is under da pillow," I said, as I pointed toward it and took a look around to make sure I wasn't leaving anything, before I fired up another blunt and walked out the door.

T'Mekico had checked into a suite at the Hotel of Hilton, about thirty miles outside of Waco; in the small town of Temple, Texas. She was making sure that no one would be able to detect or observe their every move. In which, she knew a lot of bitches couldn't wait to take her place in her man's life. And to her, it was normal, for hoes to go back and lie about shit that they seen her do, knowing damn well Cocaine Wayne wasn't believing that bullshit. And this was the first time she had ever cheated on him with anybody. To her, that was scary because she was really feeling Tear for real. His whole swagger was one of a kind, and he always came with a different approach, and that's what drew her closer to him as a person. He became her reliable source and more of a comfortdont than anything. Needless to say, but it probably has a lot to do with the fact that he lived in Houston for quite some time.

After she called Tear and gave him all the information about her whereabouts, he appeared at her doorsteps an hour later, dressed in a pair of all white Jordans, with a red and with Air Jordan velour sweat suit, holding a bottle of Dom P wrapped in a brown paper bag.

"What took you so long?" she asked the moment she opened the door and he walked past her.

"Damn!" A nigga don't get a hug or a kiss, just a straight questionnaire?" I said as I reached for her chin and pulled her lips closer to mine and took a kiss, as she closed her eyes and went along with the full motion. As I stepped back, I began, "To be truthful, I had to shower up and change clothes, if that was all right with you missy." I finished, as she turned around and took a seat on the king-size bed.

"You could of a less called and told me, that way I wouldn't be sitting around just waiting."

"You're right, my bad," I added, as I glanced down and witnessed the lovely sight of her dressed in an all black see-through, with no bra, but the matching G-string panties.

"But you know I've been waiting on your call all day my damn self," I replied, as sat the bottle of Moet' down and took a seat next to her on the bed.

"Don't you even try that, you know I had to work nigga," she added as she turned to face me, with one leg tucked under her ass.

"Shid, you had me thinking otherwise."

"Boy, don't go there, because you know what it is."

"That's understood, but at times, I still be wanting you to make more room for me."

"Tear, if I do, then what?"

"You already know what's up on my end. I done told you one too many times, it's self-explanatory."

"Yea, that's what you say now," she added as we both laid back and propped ourselves up on a pillow.

"Well, I said what I had to say about that subject, and I'ma leave it at that," I added with a senseless expression on my face, as she looked me in my eyes and placed her head on my chest, as I undid her bun, causing her hair to fall well past her shoulders, as I continued to run my fingers through its long wavy texture.

"You know, I like it when you wear your hair down."

"Ooh, do I?" she began. "You've never made any type of special request as long as we've been together."

"I shouldn't have to, because you're suppose to already know my like and dislike."

"Ooh, I know your like and dislike, all right," she replied as she bit into his right thigh, and took her hand and ran it underneath his shirt running her fingers through the lining of his six pack, causing an erection to appear through his sweat pants.

"Girl, you gonna start something you can't finish."

"Who said I can't finish?"

"We'll see about that later, did you bring the movie I asked you to bring."

"Yes, I did as a matter of a fact, so let me put it in before we get too carried away," she added with a smirk on her face, as she walked over and pushed play on the VCR. The sound of Scarface the movie came blurring out the speaker, as she dimmed all the lights and sat back down on the bed. We came to found out that that was both of our favorite movies of all times.

After I smoked a blunt and downed a few glasses of Moet', I started to feel like Tony; knowing all real niggas love Tony Montana and the way he carried his-self throughout the whole movie. His ambition and his drive to be the best in the game is what captured every niggas that was out there in these streets; living their lives turning crumbs into bricks; in which, that's real life in every ghetto and hood around the world.

Needless to say, but the females loved Scarface and his "I don't give a fuck attitude." And to T'Meikco not only was Tear a similar reflection of him, but he was the thuggish, rugged type, in whom had charisma, with a brilliant mind-set when it came down to what he really wanted out of life. His conversation and thought process always seemed to have her mind open and yearning for more. His whole demeanor and philosophy about life was to live your every day as if it's your last and play it like a game of *chess*. Strategize your every move you make before you make it.

Growing up under his terms caused him to understand that at times a person will have to give up and sacrifice something in order to conquer and get the best understanding of what life and wisdom really was.

After popcorn and the movie, things went for a change of direction. The sound of R-Kelly filled the air as we found ourselves wrapped in one another arms; engaged in a kiss that at that moment connected us to be as one.

I let my hands gently explore her entire body, causing her to flinch and giggle, as if she was still a ticklish little girl who really enjoyed every moment of the matter.

"Boy, stop that tickle," were the words that kept coming out her mouth. Until moments later, she found herself real comfortable, as I placed two nice-sized pillows underneath the small part of her back, all while removing everything except the black lace thong that hugged every inch of her frame.

In which, it wasn't long before I found myself, kissing, and licking around the lining of each of her nipples, causing them to harden on every continuation of contact. Her body was trembling and sending me every message I needed to keep going. My mission was to fulfill her by any means, and with that said, I found my tongue and lips touching, kissing, and licking every inch of her body without overlooking or abandoning a dry spot on her caramel skin. I ran my tongue around the rim of her navel, before I moved lower and begun to nibble on her inner thighs, while running the tip of my nose up and down the lining of her thong, feeling the moisture of her wetness, her juices were flowing. I could feel the warmth of her body next to mine, and the feeling was so incredible. I teased her pearl tongue through the material of her thong, all the while looking up and watching her—watching me through glossy eyes, as I removed her thong and she was completely naked. That's when, I took my tongue and slowly began to run laps around her clitoris, causing her to tilt her head, arch her back, while grabbing me by the back of my head and pulling me closer to her as she opened and closed her eyes again, with full view of every lick that sent a sensational feeling through her entire body.

My cell phone started to ring, but before I could give it any attention, she kicked it off the bed, not wanting anything to get in the way of distracting me from giving her some of the best head she has ever had in her twenty-three years of living. My tongue continued to dance to her every move, if I found a rhythm that made her toes curl, I'd stay at that pace and did that until she couldn't take it anymore.

"How does it feel?" were the words that came from my mouth.

"OOOOOOOhhhhhhhhhhh, Tear, baby, give it to me. Give me all of you!"

I just smiled as I kissed my way up her body, flipped her over, laying her face down, on her stomach, and repeated my same licking techniques once I took her ass cheeks and spread them wide open. This was driving her insane. She was worming, biting the pillow, reaching for the headboard, and moaning and breathing uncontrollable. This was the first time she has ever had her ass licked, and the feeling was something that she has yet to find the definition for. But the sensation of my warm wet tongue was making every nerve in her body jump to a beat that she never knew lived within her.

She was lying on her stomach with her ass pushed up in the air, cum running, and my entire chin was soaked in her sweetness. And the sight of watching her cum made my dick get hard as still. I straddled her from the back and co-misted to pull her hair all the while penetrating and give it all to her in my favorite doggy-style position.

She was running from the dick, and I could tell she couldn't take it all at one time; so I had to start out slow with short strokes, causing her to relax, and get in a little more, as I begun to catch the rhythm, and she started to throw it back to me. And to me, her juices were wetter than Niagara falls and that allowed me dig deeper and deeper. I took a good grab of her hair and pulled her closer, as she just opened up more and more.

We switched back into missionary, and I pulled out one of my classic moves, while sliding in and out of her with a combination of stokes; five short stokes-one long deep stoke followed by 'six short stokes-two long deep stokes, followed by 'seven short stokes-four long deep stokes, and repeated that over and over, while I took my left hand and reached up under her and worked my index finger inside her ass, and then, I took right hand and begun to rub her clit, all while I was still penetrating her with eight inches of long, rock-hard, stiff dick, sending her into a state of not really believing the excesses of knowing if she was coming or going.

"Baby, I want you on top," I said, as she snapped back to reality and took control by throwing her legs across mine, taking her hand and guided her way down, riding my dick, tossing her hair back, as the sound of "Honey Love" filled the air.

"IIIIIIImmmmmmm bout cum,"

"CCCCummmmm for me, Daddy," she said as she stop riding my manhood and stuck my entire piece into her mouth and she couldn't help, but suck me until I couldn't take it any more as I released my load into the back of her throat. As we both just laid there exhausted, sweaty, and out of breath. "I can't lie; you put it on me" were the first words to escape my mouth just as the sound of sleep filled the air of room 112.

The next morning, we were wrapped in each other arms, with last night breathe still in our mouths.

"Babe what's on the agenda for today? "I asked as I patted her on her naked ass and she turned to face me.

"It really don't matter to me. I didn't have anything to do or no one to report to for the next 24 hours."

"Is that right?" I asked as I rolled out of bed all ampped up.

"Well let's go swimming then."

"Swimming"

"Yea it's an indoor pool down stairs in the lobby." I added as she agreed. As we were turning the corner, I must admit the elements of surprise caught me off guard. I tapped T'Meikco on her shoulder, because she was looking in the other direction.

"Look" I said as she turned and seen it for herself with her own two eyes. It was the sight of Cocaine Wayne and Me-Me getting on the elevator, all hugged up, laughing, with his hands gripped tight on Me-Me ass.

"What that da fuck!" she begun as the elevator door closed shut and they continued on without knowing they had been spotted by us.

"Hell, Na'll!" she blazed out and stormed toward the elevator, causing me to reach out and grab her by the arm.

"Let me fucking go," she yelled out, drawing a scene by the hotel lobby observes.

"I'm not letting your ass go, because your ass is really tripping right now for real," I expressed as I pulled her closer to me and we were face-to-face.

"Tear, I know you just seen that shit. I can't fucking believe that bitch!" she was saying in between tears, as they began to fall eagerly.

"Come on, Meikco," I said, as I led her back into the room, and I could tell from the look on her face that she was really hurt by that incident.

"Tear, out of all the people in this world, why Meme?" she began as she put her hands over her face and pulled her knees to her chest and started crying.

"We were like sisters!"

"We've been best friends ever since elementary, and this how this bitch repay me for my loyalty!"

I just sat there rubbing her back, while she vented. I know she was really hurt and taking this to heart. All I could do was ease the moment and become the shoulder she needed to lean on, the ears that she needed to listen, and most of all, the comfort she yearned for at this point.

She leaned her head into my chest and hugged me as we laid back on the unmade bed, as I continued to rub her head and run my fingers through her hair.

"Baby, everything will be all right, I promise you!"

"How the fuck can you say something like that at a time like this!" she asked with a stare that said one thing, *kill.*

"Baby, you got me on your team" were words that eased out of my mouth, when in reality I really don't know where the statements came from or what statement should come next that would ease her pains? She lifted her head off my chest and looked me directly in the eyes. I could tell she was in a real confused state of mind.

"Tear, what do you mean I got you on my team, when you know like I know you got a girl at home right now in the blind about us, just sitting there waiting on you to decide to home."

"You still got me regardless of the fact."

"But you're not mine, you must of forgot, and plus you might not want me the way I want you."

"What type of shit is that?" I asked with a frown on my face.

"I mean I've never cheated on this nigga, not a day in the three years we've been together, until I met you and we started talking, and that bitch was the main reason that I even considered that thought and gave in. Bitch kept talking about all the hoes she done heard he was fucking and plus I know for a fact that he was cheating on me with that other bo-legged ass bitch Keshia Randolph, but all along she was fucking him too.

Just then, my cell phone started to ring, but after I seen it was from an unknown caller, I turned my ringer off, reached over, and pulled her closer to me.

"So where do we go from here?" she asked.

"You tell me, where would you prefer for us to go?"

"Tear, I'm not going back there. I refuse to, not after this bullshit."

"That's not what I asked you."

"Tear, I shouldn't have to tell you what I want, when you already know what I want, but it's all on you," she added as she broke our eye contact and drifted off into a trance.

"Tear, you know what?"

"What's that?"

"I can set Cocaine Wayne ass up, so you can rob him," she said as her whole demeanor changed, and she had a real lifeless expression on her face.

All I could say was "Yea," because it hadn't dawned on me that I really had the upper hand in this situation, and the opportunity had presented itself for me to take giant step in the game. Everybody knew this nigga was having real money, and when I looked her in the eyes, I could tell she was for real about what she just said.

"So how would you go about doing just that?" I asked. In which, I could tell she had to think on it for a minute, and she knew it was a gamble. But to me, it was fuck Cocaine Wayne and Meme, and to her, it was the same. So we were on the same page when it came down to this; and right now, her mind was made up. "I'll show them," was all she could think about as she opened her mouth and said.

"I don't know, but I know I will, it's just up to you, and I expect you to do all the planning."

"Oh, I got that and I know just how we'll do it," I began as I took full control of the conversation, while gaining all the information she could provide me with about this nigga and all his hidden treasures.

"Look, I want you to know, once this is done, you're leaving this nigga, we're packing up and moving to one or the other, Austin or Dallas, get us a house, and get you back to school, so you can finish up your RN certification like you really want to," I added giving her all the insight, vision, and security she needed to believe in me as hers truly.

"But what about Dakota?" she asked believing every word that was being spoken.

"I can handle that or I wouldn't be telling you all this. You know as it is, I really don't fuck with a lot of females, because not everybody fit my standards," I added.

"So how can we do it," she asked intensified, as I ran it down to her and let her know she had to control her actual emotions, until everything went down. She agreed to act as if she knows nothing about what she had seen, and she would play it to the tee.

She filled me in that he just went to Houston to re-up because he made a call to his connect.

"Is that how he normally does it?"

"Yea, he's usually gone for two days and then he'll come back, make a few calls, but lately, he's been complaining about a few of his workers been coming up short."

"Yea, who Nick and BT them."

"Yea."

"Where does he usually keep his work?"

"Now, that I don't know, but he keeps money inside a safe, behind the nightstand in our room."

"Okay, here's how we can solve that problem," I began to explain the setup, and made the adjustments where they were needed, and she agreed to go along as planned. I dried up her tears, and once it was all said and done, we'll be on our way. While I continued to run our enterprise, Tameikco could see Tear was capable of taking control and he could handle everything if it got out of hand. And Cocaine Wayne, Meme, and Dakota would be out of the picture. In her mind, it was fuck all of them. She had everything she's ever wanted wrapped up all in one, a real man.

"Meikco, can you handle your position?"

"I know I can," she agreed, not really believing the shit she seen with her own two eyes today. "How could pleasure become pain, within the blink of an eye," she thought to herself. To her, this was the same person, in whom ate her food when she was hungry, the only person she had ever confined in, the one who would lift her up with encouraging words and comfort when she was depressed about something that life had sent her way, and here it is, she was the same bitch who talked her into cheating and being unfaithful when she really didn't want to do the shit, but come to find out this was the same bitch that was fucking her man behind her back, and this shit just didn't sit well with her.

"I got something for their ass, and I won't be satisfied until they get what they deserve," were the thoughts running through her mind.

*   *   *

I wasted no time telling Crazy Kev and Dough-Boy to meet me at my apartment, and I could tell from their tone of voice that they were anxious to find out what's really going on.

"Nigga, your ass lying like a muthafucker!" Crazy Kev said as he took a hit on the Newport that dangled from in between his pitch black lips.

"That nigga was fucking Meme too," Dough-Boy asked as he listened to me give them a rundown about what happened at the room.

"Big Bro, I knew that bitch was a snake," Dough-Boy added with an emotionless expression on his face.

"So are you for sure she's going to set this lick-up?" Crazy Kev asked, ready to put this play into effect, so he could play his position and take care of his business.

"Yea, that's all real, a nigga just got to fill in all the blanks to make sure we have a clean get-away," I added.

"Mann, this'll put us on a whole 'nother level," Crazy Kev said as he drifted off into a daze, just thinking about it.

"Shid, that's what we hustle for anyway, so it's by any means necessary," I added, as we brought our meeting to an end.

The next day I found myself on the phone with Tameikco, all day it seemed like, and all we could talk and think about was her filling me in on what she knew her position consist of and she was ready to play it to the fullest; in which, that's what I need and I knew it was only a matter of time from this moment on.

(Chapter 13)

Club Contagious

December 2, 1996, was once again another one of those cold, wind blowing, ice breaking, winter nights. As the sun slowly disappeared, a full moon took control, and became the light that shined so far away, covering the darkness that filled the streets that has failed so many of us in our generation.

But the panoramic view of Club Contagious was in full swing of things, as the lights were flashing, bailers were valet parking their cars, as all the parking spaces were filling up, and people were all en route toward the half-a-block long wait to get in line. And it was "Lady's Night Out," one of those nights where all the locals and out of towners mixed and mingled with one another.

The underworld gave the college grads a taste of what success looked like from a hood point of view, and tonight was one of those nights that it wasn't a secret. We were in dat bitch deep, like hood superstarz do whenever you fall in on their turf. Everyone was there except Black Ty, and no one knew where he was.

"Man, where is Black Ty ass at?" I asked once we were all parked in valet, adjusting our shirts and jackets.

"The last I heard he was on his way to Killeen to serve these niggaz he was cool with," Dough-Boy said, as he continued to fix his shirt, while moving toward the front of his car.

"That what he told me too, last night," Crazy Kev added.

"Yea, that was last night," Dough-Boy said as he looked up and finished tucking and fluffing his shirt out to fit his approval.

"Shid, his ass probably down there laying up letting one of those half-breed hoes, letting da bitch suck his dick for her rent, and ride his face for a new living suit," I added as we all laughed and mobbed our way toward the main entrance, bypassing this mile-long ass line. But you know, money talk, and playing the wait in line game was out of our league. We spoke and threw the deuce to a few females that we knew from around our way, as we could feel the cold stares from those that observed us from afar and only wish they could be part of our entourage, but can't, and we continued to step forward.

"A look, I got all of ya'll, so come on," Crazy Kev was saying as he pointed at a crowd of females, in whom they all jumped out of line and rushed to the front and followed his lead. He paid everybody way and we kept it moving. The closer we got to the bar I could see all the major players. One of the youngest playa's in game was doing just what he do best, throwing money in the air.

"What's up, baby boy?" I said, as we greeted one another with a smile that said a million respectful words.

"Shid, you know me Big Homie. A nigga making it rain hundred dollar bills, and giving these hating ass niggas a chance to eat the crumbs off my table," he added as he just threw the rest of the one hundred bills he had in his hand in the air, and smiled. This was one young nigga who had style about his-self, and he was one the few that had the heart of a real, live, diehard hustler, and knew just how to go out and get it. When everyone else chose to sell crack, this nigga did the opposite and sold heroin, and was raking in all the money, and that's what most niggas respected about him.

Everyone else just enjoyed the moment and popped bottle after bottle, giving love to one another. It was one of those highlighted moments, and it felt good to be in the midst of living life around nothing but real niggaz with real live money. East Side was deep in that bitch, and niggaz were still strolling in.

"What's up, my nigga?" Tuna-Fish yelled out from across the table, as I reached out. We gave one another a certified eastside handshake and sat down at the round table with a few more of my homeboys

"What's up, Boocee and Lil Chris, baby?" I added when I seen my other two potnaz walk up to the table and take a sit talking about the two baylor hoes they just pulled.

"Look out, Tear, baby, what kind of drink you boyz want?" Odis called out as he held up this super fine ass Asian waiter, and within minutes, she was walking back with a tray of two bottles of Gray Goose and two bottles of Malibu coconut-flavored Caribbean rum followed by another waiter carrying a jug of cranberry Juice and six nice, sparkling, tall, iced,-up wine glasses.

"Miss, if you don't mind, I would like a round of Cristal for these two tables," Dough-Boy called out as he sat back down, and we all just watched the club watch us from a sideline point of view.

The waiter then came back and passing out bottles of Cristal, as if it was H20. Don Juan, the owner of the club came over and greeted us with nice firm handshake.

Lil James returned his handshake and whispered something that made him walk over to the DJ booth and fill in whatever the request may have been.

The DJ then turned the music down and his deep, husky voice filled the club.

"This goes out to all the lovely young ladies and the whole eastside family. The big boss has just informed me that the back bar has been bought for the next thirty minutes, so drink up as I play this one song and give all you real niggaz a real reason to lift your glass up and toast to all the real niggaz that lost their lives in these heartless streets." And that statement was followed by the classic sound of "One day here and the Next day Gone," a rap song written by UGK, and the sound just set the mode, as we all stood up and bobbed our heads to the beat as the voice of DJ Red-Man began.

"Look out Waco, I need you boyz to work with me. Let's have a moment of silent for all our fallen soldiers that the Good Lord has called upon to watch over us, as we continue to live our lives to the fullest. Hold your cups up high and give a toast for these boys Osman, Lil E., Big G-Wayne, Lil Bookie, Lil Wesley, Yoshema, Lil Jimmy T., Lil Gary, Big G., P. T., Boo, and last but not least to dat boy T-Maine. These were some of the few that really made a compact in our lives, rather you know it or not. So may they all REST in PEACE. I know the list goes on, but let's enjoy ourselves because it's real out here in theses streets. The least expected can and will always happen, just mark my word."

Serious expression covered the faces of almost every hood nigga that knew the story behind the names that the DJ had just called out. The whole *eastside* had their cups held up high and gave a real legendary toast rapped every word to the song.

And it was one of those moments where you realize that you really had a homeboy that you miss, and it's understood that you'll never ever see alive again, at less not on this side of the God's green earth. Because no matter how hard you think about it, tomorrow will never be promised and you'll never know when you're time has come, until the moment reveals itself, and you're the main topic in the streets' newspaper, written by your local street news reporter.

Just then, I felt a tap on my shoulder that caused me to turn around and the sight of Cocaine Wayne definitely caught me off guard, and brought me back to reality.

"Young Tear, what's up, fam?" he asked as he reached out his hand for me to shake it. I did; all the while I'm looking and searching for his full intention for tapping on me and not knowing really had me off balance and on high alert. I could see out of my peripheral view that Dough-Boy had informed Crazy Kev; as they both stood up and inched in closer.

"What's up with you, my nigga?" I replied while observing his every move, searching for his motive.

"Shid, I'm trying to holla at you for a minute, with a small business proposition."

"Right now, I'm chilling, but what's on your mind?"

"Shid, I keep money on my mind at all times and right now, I want to know what your price on a ticket is? So I can see if I can match it or beat it," he shot back as he leaned in and lowered his tone of voice.

"Well, that just depends on what type of deal you got for me and my family?" I stated just to see what angle this nigga was really coming from, for real.

"I might want to help you out and make life a little more comfortable for the both of us," was his response as we locked eye contact.

"Well, shid, my nigga, let's exchange numbers and talk about this under different circumstances."

"Let's do just that, and I'm willing to meet you halfway."

"Well, that's what's up. Shit sounds good to me, but I want you to know it's a lot of things I don't play with, and my money is one of 'em, so keep it one hundred with me, and we might be able to put something into motion," I said as I looked him directly in his eyes, not really believing my stroke of good luck. In which, I'ma play it how it go and let everything fall into place. These were the thoughts that ran through my head, as a numb gut feeling shifted through my body, as we exchanged numbers and made plans to meet one another the next day.

Later on that night, I gave Dough-Boy and Crazy Kev a full rundown of our conversation. I called T'Meikco and gave her the news to let her know that tomorrow just might be the day, if everything goes right. We should be moving in forward progress.

(CHAPTER 14)

The Round Table

"Chess"
Every Real Hustler's Dream.

It was a little past three o'clock in the afternoon, as Me, Dough-Boy, and Crazy Kev were all posted up inside room 214 at the Brazos Inn Hotel with well over fifty-one thousand dollars counted out in cash, inside our hotel room. We discussed, strategized, and went over our plan carefully, making sure every inch of detail had been covered as everybody knew the position they were to play.

I had just hung the phone up with Cocaine Wayne, and we had worked out a deal where he had agreed to serve me three bricks for my money; in which, immediately the round table meeting was called upon as our minds came together, and we got ready for whatever the case may bring.

I sat my tan and brown Gucci backpack full of armor on the table, and tossed my Baylor Bears fitted cap on the bed.

"Man, where the fuck is Black Ty?" Crazy Kev asked.

"Shid, still ain't heard from him since he went to Killeen," I said as they both shook their heads.

"I called his phone, but still no answer, so I don't know what's up with that."

"Nigga ass still fresh out and this nigga want to fuck everything in sight."

92

"Well, fuck it, we'll catch up with him later! We got business to take care of, ya-dig," I said as I begun to pull out everything from the backpack.

"All right, here's the full layout," I added as I got each ones attention.

"Now, Crazy Kev, I want you to take the stash car and park it in front of Aunt Lynn's house and make sure you leave the keys in the ashtray and the doors unlocked, that way when I switch cars, I won't have a problem getting into it," I added as I turned and pointed at Dough-Boy.

"Look, you follow Crazy Kev, and I want ya'll to post up at that store on the corner of Waco Drive and Turner Street." As I looked each man in their eyes and realized they were ready for whatever, we all agreed. I tossed each one a pair of all black icier-tone gloves while placing a pair inside the back pocket of my kinaki pants.

"Here, you take this," I added, as I thrust a smoke gray, charcoal-colored P89 Ruger toward Dough-Boy. He immediately grabbed it by its handle, examined it, and smiled. I could see the excitement in his eyes because he had the heart of a lion, and he couldn't wait to turn a nonbeliever into a cold, firm, and stiff believer.

"Big Bro with no weapons, no witness, and no clues, there's nothing them laws can do," he added as he just played and looked at the gun as if was a toy.

"Yea, I know, and it's a must we all come back together in one piece," I said as I pushed Crazy Kev an all chrome Desert Eagle.

"Here, cuddy, you take the forty and make sure all the finger prints are wiped clean," I ordered, as I took the Mac-11 with the shoulder strap and swung it across my shoulder.

"Now, I want you two niggaz to listen to me and listen to me good. This is it baby, and there's no turning back from here, so let's go take care of our business and get this money."

"Cuddy, have you talked to T'Meikco?"

"Yea, everything's set up the way we've planned it. She knows what position I need her in. Matter of a fact, she called right before I came over and said he was at the barber shop," I finished as I placed the fifty-one thousand dollars inside a McDonald's bag. I stuffed it in my backpack as I picked up my cell phone and listened until I heard the sound of Cocaine Wayne's voice come through my speakers.

"What's up, my nigga," I spoke into the phone.

"Shid, you already know what it is on my end. I'm just sitting back waiting on you," Cocaine Wayne said as he thought about the conversation they had earlier. He knew Tear and his family was some young niggaz about their money and that's what he needed on his team because ever since him and his younger brother moved back from Houston, the streets been watchin' 'em, and it was only a matter of time before everything just fell into place.

"So where you at?" I asked as my heart started beating from the adrenaline rush, along with the anticipation of hoping everything go the way we expected.

"I'm at the shop. About how long will it take before you come this way?"

"About twenty minutes, I'll be headed that way," I added, as I looked at Dough-Boy and Crazy Kev and winked.

"That's what's up. I'll be here waiting on you."

"Bet that," I said as flipped the phone shut and reached for my fitted cap.

"Okay, look, here's the play," I began, as I stuck my cell phone inside my pocket, and put my fitted cap back on top of my head.

"He's at the shop, so I want you two to be in the position to see everything. And once I pull off from the barber shop, I want one of ya'll to call me, and don't leave the post until he leave, because you two are going to follow him."

"Where will the deal go down?" Crazy Kev asked

I'ma make it go down at Church's on Clifton Street. I'll call if that change, so ya'll follow him, just like we've practiced, and from there, he should lead ya'll straight to the dope.

"Crazy Kev, make sure you follow his every move, and once he comes back and serve me, I'm going to give him the fifty-one thousand dollars, and hope he take it back home. But that's where T'Meikco comes in at, because she do know where the money is, but she don't have the combination to the wall safe where he keeps majority of his money, but we'll get him to open that up with ease. It's either the money or his death, and it's that simple."

"Or we just do both, fuck it," Dough-Boy said as he inhaled the smoke from a Newport that he was smoking.

"Either way, we got to make sure everything go as planned," I added as we all stood up and walked toward the door and looked at one another.

"Well, this is it baby," Crazy Kev said as we all walked out the door.

*   *   *

On my way down the stairs, I hit the button on my remote and the driver-side door swung open as the V8 LTL engine started with a roar. I just sat behind the wheel of a 1996 SS Impala, zoned out, en route to what could become a real life-changing event. And for a change, I decided not to smoke a blunt before I met up with dude, because for real I knew I needed a clear mind in this situation.

The silence of the car made me sink into a real deep meditation. Where all I could think about was the amount of dope and money we could possible have before the clock strike midnight tonight. This was the opportunity every Hustla dreamed and wondered about, and it just fell in my lap. And by me being the risk taker that I am, I took full advantage of it and said fuck it, I'm all for it, knowing this could have a flip side to it, but fuck it; we're here now, so let's play it how it goes; and get it how you live. "All or nothing," was the last thought that ran through my mind as I pressed play on the Alpine and the sound of 2Pac came deafening out the woofers. I started rapping along with the song, bobbing my head; just when my cell-phone started ringing. I turned the music down and answered. It was voiced operated, saying something about a collect call from a Federal Inmate.

"Inmate, state your name."

"Black Ty!"

"Press five to accept or hung up to deny it."

As I pressed five, I couldn't believe this shit; this nigga ass done went to jail.

"Mann, what the fuck your ass doing in jail?" were the first words that came flying out of my mouth.

"What the fuck you mean you caught a FED case?" I yelled into the phone, not believing the words that just ran through my ears and what my nigga was really saying to me.

"So how much is your bond?" I asked, as I listened and he told me that he was being held on a federal No bond.

"Well, look, I'm go talk to a lawyer and see what he has to say, but do you have any money on your books?" I asked, as he filled me in about the FEDs confiscating the $9,377 that he had in his pocket and was going to use it for some kind of evidence against him.

"Nigga, I've never heard of no shit like that, but don't trip. You'll have a stack on your books sometime tonight. If not, tomorrow for sure," I added as we continued to talk. He filled me in on what happened and how it all went down. Then, our call was disconnected, and I was in a state of shock.

"I told that nigga about fucking with these niggaz he really don't know, they'll get your ass every time, and he still took his ass to Killeen to sale work," I thought to myself as I picked up the phone and called Dough-Boy, but got a busy signal; so I called Crazy Kev.

"Where ya'll at?" I asked once I heard him pick the phone up.

"We already posted up, the stash cars parked, and now we're just sitting waiting on you."

"That's what's up, a' nigga have you heard about what happen to Black Ty?"

"Yea, Dough-Boy on the phone with him now, and that's fucked up."

"He called me just minute ago, but we'll worry about that shit later. Let's take care of this other shit," I said as I came to the red light on Waco Drive and Dallas Street. I clicked the phone off and laid it down in the passenger seat.

Once the light turned green and I passed Dough-Boy and Crazy Kev up, I hit my blinker and made a left turn on Hood Street and pulled into the parking lot of Cocaine Wayne's Beauty and Barber Shop, and it wasn't long before he came out and took a seat inside my car.

"Damn, baby, I like this muthafucker right here!" he said as he looked around and checked out the inside of my car. I could tell he was impressed by the customized seventeen-inch Clarion touch-tone screens falling from the baseboard, hanging right behind the headrest of the driver and passenger seat; wood grain was wrapped throughout the car, the dash, door panels, and steering wheel all had matching wood.

"How much you pay for these screens?"

"I got a good deal from my peoples in the city."

"Yea, that's what's up, I'm thinking about putting my drop in the shop, and pulling it back out this summer."

"Shid, I can take you to these Mexicanz, that paint and customize all my shit and you gonna love these boyz for real my nigga. Just watch and see how I come down, turning heads this summer and hurt these boyz. My shit almost ready right now as we speak but I'ma wait to break these boyz off like it's suppose to be done."

"I'm feeling that Young Tear baby, and I'ma make sure we do just that," Lil Cocaine Wayne replied, as I took control of the conversation and switched the subject to the real reason why we were sitting here.

"That's a must, whenever you get ready, but what's up on the issue doe?"

"Shid, ain't nothing changed, it's like I said this morning, I got whatever; I just want you to play Straight up with me, and we can do business with one another all the time., Cocaine Wayne explained as he sat back and reclined on the buck-hive seats.

"That's what's up, but me personally, I play with all my money on the wood, up front, and right now I'm trying to cop three bricks with no games to be played." I said as I glanced at this chick walking by, holding a little boy's hand leading him inside the barbershop.

"Okay, my nigga, I can feel that and that's not a problem," Cocaine Wayne added knowing he needed real niggas like Tear on his team, so he could leave all these other po-hustling ass niggz alone. He needed young hungry niggaz that grinded super hard and chased paper like it was going out of style. Cause for real living, life without money, is like living life without oxygen to breathe. In which, it was hard to find young niggaz, who understood the drive of going out and getting real life money, the kind that it takes hours to count. The kind that after you finished counting it, you will put a smile on your face sssssooooooooo fucking big, you'll just stare at it. It gives you that feeling like you done conquered the whole entire world, and Cocaine Wayne seen that in these young niggaz. They had the hearts of old niggaz in the game and that's what you need on your team, in this day and age.

"Tear, let's say I serve you for the three bricks and then put two more on top of that for consignment."

"Sound like a real live game plan that I'm cool with, but how soon are so expecting for me to bring the other thirty-two thousand dollars back, cause on the real, I move at my own pace. But it's one thing for sho', if I do decide to take you up on that offer, your piece of change, comes off the top, and that's real!"

"Young Tear, I can dig that, and that's what's up, because it's enough money out here for the both of us, so it's all on you, it's whatever on my end."

"Well, that's what the business is then," I added, as I reached over the back seat, grabbed the backpack, sat it in my lap, and unzipped it.

"I just you want you to know it's all real with me, my nigga," I said as took the McDonald's bag from the backpack and showed him fifty-one thousand dollars, folded in thousand-dollar stacks.

At that moment, a blind man could see the greed lingering around inside his eyes. In which, the sight made me think of what this old playa use to always tell me. He would state that "One honest and sincere move can cover up over a dozen dishonest moves, so always play pussy get fucked when you're dealing with anybody outside your inner circle, because those are the ones you'll really need in this ice-cold, dirty world."

And now it's as if I really understood just what he was telling me at that time. A smoke screen was always used to hide your intentions, while giving you enough time to seal any deal.

"Young Tear, I know you're ready and that's what I like about you and your fam; so just give me about thirty minutes and we'll meet up at?"

"Shid, we'll meet at Church's." I said picking a wide-open location to keep Dough-Boy and Crazy Kev in plain view of everything going on.

"That's a bet, my nigga, let me take care of my business, and I'll call you when I'm on my way," he said as we brought our deal to closure and went our separate ways. I pulled off just thinking and hoping our plan B go just as well as plan A.

As of right now, everything was really looking lovely. But only God knew the destiny of the mission we were on, I thought to myself as I reached and grabbed my cell phone, while placing a headset on head and called T'Meikco.

"Hello," was the sound of her soft spoken voice, as it came whispering through my headset. I adjusted the volume to hear the words that she spoke.

"What are you doing?" I asked.

"I'm just sitting here, waiting on your phone call, so fill me what's up."

"Well, I want you to know that today is the day, so stay posted and don't move unless I tell you otherwise."

"I got this, you just make sure you do this shit right and we get away with it, because I didn't want anything to happen to you or your brother them."

"Baby, we got this, so don't worry, everything is under full control, but look, I'll call you back. I just wanted fill you in and let you to know that it's about to go down, so be ready, because from this point on, it's me and you against the world."

"I got you, baby. I'm just ready to get this shit over with and move forward," she said sounding as serious as she could be, taking out all the resentment in her voice.

"It's almost over, baby. So don't worry. Dreams are about to be made reality," I replied as I ended her call and called Crazy Kev on his cell phone.

"Talk to me, cuddy," he said as soon as he answered the phone.

"Look, I want you boyz to know that it's a go, so make sure you follow that nigga the moment he pull off from that parking lot."

"I got that Big cuddy. The nigga just hopped inside his car, so we'll call you back in a minute," Crazy Kev said once he seen Cocaine Wayne come out the barber shop, and walked toward his car and got in.

After about ten minutes of trailing him, Crazy Kev and Dough-Boy could tell that these nigga was headed toward Bellmead, a real small town about fifteen minutes outside of Waco.

He clicked his blinker and emerged from Interstate 35, while exiting Meyers Lane, and made the first right turn, then another left turn, before his car came to a complete stop and pulled into the driveway of a big ass two-story red brick house, with a navy blue L. S Lexus parked in the driveway.

"Ain't dat old girl car?" Dough-Boy asked as he squinted his eyes for a better look down the street.

"Shid, it looks like it."

"Call Tear, and let him know where we're at." Dough-Boy told Crazy Kev as he picked up the phone and speed dialed Tear's number.

Tear couldn't believe what he just heard. To him it was like killing two birds with one stone! he thought, as he then told them follow Cocaine Wayne and get ready to set up the next move.

But just as he hung up the phone with them, T'Meikco called in a shaky voice and said, "Tear, Cocaine Wayne just left and he's on his way to meet you."

"All right, but look, I want to watch the clock and call him at exactly four forty-five on the dot. Tell him that you need some money to go buy a few things and just make up some shit.

"Once he come back, make sure you have the side door that leads into the kitchen is unlock, and I want you to be in the kitchen when I come through, and everything will be over before you know."

"Okay, baby, I got it. Don't forget to make this look good. All right?"

"I will, baby, just let me handle this."

"I am,." ahe said as she paused and the line got real quite.

"Tear."

"What's up. Look before you start, I want you to know I got this under control, so don't' worry about a thang."

"I'm not worried. I just wanted to tell you that I really do love you, from the bottom of my heart, and that's all I wanted to say."

"Meikco, that's something I already know, and you know just how I feel about you, don't you?"

"Yes I do, and I want all this to work out."

"It will, so make sure you do exactly like I told you all right."

"I will."

"Well, it's only a matter of time, just work with me is all I ask," was my reply just as my other line started to beep.

It was Cocaine Wayne.

"Baby, I'ma call you right back; this him, and don't forget four forty-five on the dot." I said as I clicked over and answered.

"What's up fam?" I answered waiting to hear just what was on his mind.

"Shid, everything is everything. Right now, I'm on my way to get me some chicken, what about you?"

"Yea, that's what's up, I just pulled up, so I'm already posted."

"Well, I'll see you in a few."

"Bet that," I replied just as the line went dead. At that moment, my heart seemed to skip beats for some strange reason. Both of my hands were starting to create sweat, and my mind was racing with all types of thoughts.

Then, the time had presented itself, and I realized that it was no turning back. His SUV had pulled up and parked next to me. I glanced down at my watch; it read (4:37 p.m.), as I got out, took a look around and spotted Crazy Kev and Dough-Boy watching my every move as I got inside the SUV.

I had over fifty thousand dollars on me, and I needed everything to fall in place without a mistake being made. These were the thoughts that ran through my head, as I sat down and closed the door to his expedition.

"I got you, my nigga," were his exact words as he reached behind him and grabbed a brown HEB grocery bag and set it in his lap and opened it. I reached in and grabbed a block, ran my test on each one, and gave him the McDonalds Bag; as he looked at the money, we both left a sign of relief that no one was trying to fuck over the other one.

"Is it all here?"

"Hell, yea, and it's all in one hundred dollar bills."

"That's what's up, well, shid, my nigga, as long as we can continue to play straight up with one another, we won't have any problems, ya dig."

"You already know, what it is on my end," I replied as we sealed the deal just as his phone rang at four forty-five on the dot. And all I heard him say was "All right, I was on my way back that way anyhow," and flipped his phone, as we shook one another hands.

"Give me about four dayz, and I'll give you a call for da rest of that change."

"Bet that, my nigga. You boyz take it easy out there, and call me if you have a problem with anything."

"That's what's up," I added, as I took a look around to make sure the coast was clear and hopped out of his Expedition and got back into my car.

Everything was going as planned, and I couldn't believe just how this nigga was so easy to predict. Made me think I should have been a stickup kid, instead of a dope-boy.

But then again; that robbing shit wasn't for me, and it drew too much attention. It's hard to make it when you have too many arch enemies, because you can't get money comfortable. You either get money or you take the world to war, because it's hard to do both, without slipping.

And we live in a world where slipper count. So make sure you choose one or the other, whenever that time presents itself.

"To me, this nigga team really don't consist of certified street niggas. These were a bunch of school boyz that somehow ran into a connection that took them above and beyond. And it is what it is," were the thoughts that ran through my mind as I called my aunt Stacey Lynn's house.

"Hello." she answered

"A there, big head."

"Boy, what do yo ass want?"

"I'm on my way over there, and I'm coming to park my car in the back of your driveway," I said as I was turning down the street that she lived on.

"Alright, I'll be here." She replied knowing dat her favorite nephew had one or two things going on when he called her to park his car.

One, he was either hiding from his girlfriend and didn't want to be detected; or, two, he was back to dealing that shit again.

In which, she hated to see their younger generation go down the same routes that her brothers had taken, as well as their daddies had taken, but she never asked them about their business, and neither did she ever want to know about it, That was their lives, and she wanted them to live it to the fullest.

I parked the car, put a car cover over it, and jumped inside the stash car all the while calling T'Meikco.

"Baby, he just pulled up, and yes, everything is ready, so come on!" was all she said before she hung the phone up without hesitation.

That made me call Crazy Kev and got their location.

Once we were all together, we parked inside the alley behind their house and walked toward the side door. Before I entered, I could see

T'Meikco standing above the kitchen sink, as if she was washing dishes. I reached for the door and tried it.

"It's open," I whispered, as we all stood at the door, guns drawn. Her head turned as I twisted the knob and came through the door. She seen it was me and smiled.

"Where he at?" I asked, as Crazy Kev and Dough-Boy pulled down their ski-mask and stood behind me.

"He just went inside the bedroom," she whispered back.

"All right, we got to make this shit look real, so turn around," I explained as I grabbed her from behind and eyeballed the gun in my hand.

"It ain't loaded," I lied as we made our way in front of the bedroom door. And to witness this nigga, bent down, putting stacks of money inside their wall safe. And that just made my heart start beating real fast again. Dough-Boy and Crazy Kev came from around me, guns aimed.

"Bitch, you bet not move!" Crazy Kev said in a real, deep, lion-like growl.

You could tell from the look of his eyes that he knew what it was, but wasn't ready to accept that somehow he had got caught slipping.

"Nigga, put ya hands up, and back away from the safe," Dough-Boy yelled as Cocaine Wayne complied and moved, all the while looking toward T'Meikco, as she cried with a loaded Mac11 aimed straight to her head.

"Cuddy, get the money," Dough-Boy ordered, as Crazy Kev took a pillowcase off a pillow on the bed and cleaned out the safe, and grabbed the McDonalds bag off the nightstand and threw that in too.

"Nigga, you know what it is, so do yourself a favor and give us what we came here for," I advised him ominously.

T'Meikco's hollering made us take a good look at her ass, not really knowing if she was for real and sincere. Everyone else was stuck and trapped in a daze, but the sound of Cocaine Wayne voice brought us back to our correct state of mind.

"P-P-Pl-Please," he blubbered.

"I'll tell you where it is, just don't kill or hurt us."

"Where is it then nigga, before somebody get hurt for real!" Crazy Kev added, as he kicked his foot.

"It's in the garage."

"Where at in the garage, nigga?"

"Look inside the backseat of that car. The key to it is under the front wheel, on the passenger side," he added just before Crazy Kev slapped him again and yelled to me.

"Cuddy, go check it out." As I ran and looked where he said to look and found a hidden treasure. The kind that every dope boy in America been hustling for, and right before my eyes was something that I had never seen before. A duffle bag full of birds; I grabbed it, threw across my shoulder, and walked into the room.

"I got it, it's all here." And as soon as I finished my statement, everything was in slow mode. Dough-Boy spit flame into T'Meikco's chest, causing her body to drop to the floor, killing her on contact, while her eyes remained open staring directly at me. Cocaine Wayne eyes widened at the sight of watching her body lay there limp, and then Crazy Kev let the Desert Eagle rip his skull open with two close-range shots.

"Come on, let's get out of here," Dough-Boy yelled as if he didn't see the shit that I was looking at. I just stood there stunned at the sight.

"This had to be death at its best."

"Come on, cuddy, and grab their cell phone," Crazy Kev yelled, as I came back to reality, did as instructed, and we went out the same way we came in, but as fast as we could.

(CHAPTER **15**)

Who Did This?

The Crime Scene of the Year

The once pitch-black street was now illuminated by the arrival of police cars. As Detective Sims and his partner James was assigned to the location, and now, they moved around the crime scene slowly, trying to get a real idea of what really happened. It was a known fact that two individuals were dead, and somebody had to know something.

Somehow, the news reporter got word of the killing, and now, the radio stations and even the television personnel were pulling up in record time, searching for the latest. Detective James stared at the crowd of people angrily. "How in the hell are we supposed to work on this case, he wondered, with so many fucking people in our way?" A newspaper reporter from one of the daily papers came up bearing down on him.

"Hey, Detective James," the man called out, "wait up, I have a few questions I would like to ask you."

Det. James stopped and waited patiently for the man to catch up.

"What can I do for you?" he asked as the man came in closer.

"Excuse me, can you give me a brief rundown on just what happened in that house tonight?"

"I'll be right back," Det. Sims said to his partner, as he headed toward the front door of the house. He scanned the room, adjusting his glasses on his nose. The scene was a scene, he had only seen on TV or in a movie, but not in a small town like Waco. This was an execution-style murder, where the female body was slumped over in the corner, lifeless, eyes still open, stuck in a frozen stare; whereas the male figure was still duct taped to a chair, with the remains of his brains lying on the oriental rug up under him.

"So who do you think did this?" Det. James asked his partner, as walked over toward him. Det. Sims straightened up. "Well, to me it looks to drug related, because that' Leonard Harris; you know Cocaine Wayne, the guy the FEDs been asking us about, that's him right there and that's his girlfriend T'Meikco Michigan, and the way it looks, either he hadn't paid his bills with the big man or the little men was hungry and made him the prey," he replied studying his partner closely.

"Yea, I knew this was their house, the moment we turned on this street," Det. James said as he glanced around the room searching for any sort of clues.

As the night wore on, the men working became angrier. The newspaperman and television crews were in the way everywhere the detectives turned, until tempers were ready to flare.

Det. Sims and James worked in silence inside the couples bloody bedroom. The opening of the safe was a dead giveaway that read roberry in bold letters.

"Bingo!" Sims said as he pointed toward the safe door that was left wide open.

"I want prints off everything in this room!" James ordered all the forensic that were standing around the room, just looking as if they were lost in time.

"Fuck it, we'll get 'em ourselves!" James said to his partner as they stared around the room and seen the lifeless body, one still wrapped in duct tape and the other one lying in the corner, eyes wide open. Pictures were being taken, as Sims came walking slowly behind his partner; who was walking with his head down, ignoring everything as he walked around examining the entire room. Both detectives were deep in thought, when neither men bothered to break the silence. A cold-blooded murder like this didn't make sense to Det. James, as he prayed quietly that they would catch the low-life dirtbag that committed the crime, as soon as possible.

"Well, what do you think?" Det. Sims asked, as he patted his partner on the back.

"What do I think? Mann, I haven't had the time to do such a thang. You know, all my thoughts are cloudy right now, because I really don't know what to think. All I know is that the people responsible for this musta had a real motive to kill two people like this; duct tapped up, mutiplh gun shot wounds to both victims; I mean people just don't go around killing people like this for no apparent reason. This is a' senseless as it gets," he added as he pointed around the room, and then dropped his head when his eyes came in contact with the female body covered in blood, with her eyes still open. As far as they could see, they were right back to where they began, but yet in still, they had two new deaths to add to Waco Texas's highest crime rate ever; it was 1997. Each individual had been shot dead, and the only witness they had were the walls that never told the story. They had no murder weapons, no witness, and no clues. And the evidence that they had gathered at the scene wasn't enough to shine light on who was really behind this act of street justice.

As the two men walked toward their car, they spotted the police commissioner, standing right beside the diver-side door, giving an interview to the television reporter who had confronted Det. James beforehand. Both men just continued walking until they reached their own, unmarked, tan Grand Marquis, climbed in and sat there. Each man was in his own set of deep thoughts. Both were extremely tired from the long night, of only a few hours of sleep, searching for clues to the most deadly double homicide in Waco Texas's history.

"Well, James, where do we go from here?"

"Shid, your guess is as good as mine," he said in a real soft tone of voice, before adding, "I would say, let's ride through the villa and shake up some noise, but where do we start or who do we start with," James stated as if he was lost for real, and didn't know where to start.

"Man, call a few of your informants, and maybe something will pop up, that a way," Sims said, as he started the car and pulled away from the curb.

"At less that should give us something to go on," he replied as made a right turn and emerged onto Interstate 35. As they rode in silence, the night had been too much for both men. Each one was used to violence, but not to this degree.

"You know what Sims?" James finally said as he turned to face his partner; "What we need to do is, get a hold of some of this dope pushers, and maybe one of them will know something," he finished, as he just stared at his partner to see how he was taking his idea.

"And just how do you think we should go about doing just that," Sims replied as he gathered all his thoughts and took a long deep breath. Det. James just smiled in the dark, because to him he felt as if he was onto something and he could feel it within. Det. Sims was the first black man he had ever worked with; in which, before he even came onto the force, he had doubt about working with a Black man, but somehow they reached a point where he wouldn't feel right working with anybody else. If the Waco Police Department was to break the two of them up at this moment, he knew he would have a hard time trying to readjust. For some reason, the two men just clicked tight together to the point where they took their wives out together, and of course, people would stare at them, but both men was well past that stage, and the cold stares didn't bother them in form or fashion.

"Well, first let's go in and finish up whatever paperwork we have, and then take the rest of the night off. That way, we'll have all our thoughts together."

"That sound cool with me, and I'll go let the big boss know just what it is that we're doing, so he'll know that we're working damn a double shift to crack this case; and then maybe he'll switch us to the afternoon shift. That way, we won't be burning the candles on both ends," Det. James stated as he made his exit the freeway onto Waco Drive. He didn't have to wait for his partner to okay his decision, because men understood one another way too well for that.

*   *   *

"Damn, cuddy, we did it this time!" Crazy Kev was saying as he shook his head and stared at the biggest piles of money his eyes had ever seen. Dough-Boy dumped out on the bed; and tossed the duffle bag across the room, causing it to land inside the far left-hand corner.

"Nigga, dis is a whole lot of muthafucking money, and I know Tear can't wait to run his hands through it," Dough-Boy mumbled as he glanced at the profit for leaving two people dead, with no way of returning unless it's in another lifetime, because it damn sho won't be in this one. He thought as a smile came across his face, before adding, "Crazy Kev, mann, money is a muthafucker ain't it, because a nigga can't live life without it, regardless of how you look at it."

"Yea, and the things a nigga will do to go out and get it."

"Nigga, it's real out here in these streets, living life is experience, and money is hard to come by. And I feel that we're the team to benefit from another man's lost," Dough-Boy said without a remorseful tone in his voice, both men fell silent.

Crazy Kev taking a long deep puff from the blunt they were smoking on, and blew the smoke though his nose.

"Damn, where Tear ass at?" Crazy Kev asked as he passed the blunt to Dough-Boy.

"Give 'em a minute. He'll be here. Knowing him, he probably making sure he's not being followed or he might just be caught up in traffic right now too," Dough-Boy said as he picked up a pile of cash and started counting.

"Come on, cuddy, let's put this in ten thousand dollars' stacks."

"All right, but let me go take a shit first," Crazy Kev said as he made his way toward the restroom.

"Ol' shitty ass, nigga, let me found out, you shitted on yourself."

"Nigga, fuck you!"

And after about fifteen minutes of silence, Dough-Boy's cell phone started ringing. He paused in between counts and answered.

"Talk to me."

"I'm on the stairs," was the reply from the voice breathing into the phone, before it went dead. In which, Dough-Boy stood up, walked toward the door, and peeped out the peep hole, and Tear appeared to be in front of the door, but once he seen the peep hole covered up, he turned his back to send the signal that the coast was clear. Dough-Boy unlocked the door, as Tear just stared him in the eyes without saying a word, until he reached the table where he was just sitting.

"Where's Crazy Kev?" he asked as stared at the money stationed on the table and the pile lying across the bed.

"He's in there, taking a shit."

"Nigga, you know, you two niggas wrong."

"Wrong, about what?" Dough-Boy fired back, with his face all frowned up.

"Bitch, who said to kill them?"

"I did nigga, fuck that bitch, she knew too much, and I didn't trust her, so that why I fired the first shot," Dough-Boy said as he never took his eyes off his oldest brother, the one he looked up to, the one he loved like no other, but right now, it wasn't the time to be all sensitive.

"Nigga, I don't give a damn about all that other shit. All we came to do was to get the dope and the money, not to fucking kill two muthafucking people, but na'll, you want to do shit your own way."

"Big Bro, that shit done now, so what. We can't bring 'em back, so fuck it, why we still talking about it."

Tear knew his little brother was right, and for them to continue talking about it, temper were about to start flaring and it would get all out of proportion.

"Cuddy, what took you so long?" Crazy Kev asked as he came out of the restroom, wiping his hands with a towel.

"I had to put up the work, all by myself, and that took a minute; but everything's in order now. I stashed five keys at aunty's house, in which we're going to leave them there for now as a backup plan."

"We need to go over our whole game plan, and get this shit set up, the way it's suppose to be," Tear said as they all took a seat at the table and stared at both piles of money.

"But first let's finish counting this money, and see just how much it really is," Tear added; as he ran his hands through both piles of money.

"Cuddy, hit the play button on the VCR," Dough-Boy told Crazy Kev, as he complied and the sound of Scarface came blurring through the speakers. As they bound their heads, started counting, and laid stacks of money across the table.

And if these walls had ears, it was about to hear a plan discussed amongst a family of two brothers and a cousin. Thirty thousand dollars in cash counted out already, and a whole another pile that was just waiting to be counted.

"So cuddy, what's up?" Crazy Kev asked Tear in between counts.

"We got to think this shit out to the max, with no hesitation, and just that simple."

"That way, we all stay on the same level," Dough-Boy shot back, as Tear just stared at him.

"Nigga, your ass be the only one who wants to do as you please."

"I don't want to hear about that shit no more. What's done is done," Dough-Boy added as Crazy Kev just stood there zoned out in a daze, knowing it was best to just stay out the shit, unless it was necessary.

"Cuddy, fuck that shit. Dough-Boy have a point. We can't do shit about it, so fuck it, we'll deal with that shit whenever it comes about," Crazy Kev said as he wiped sweat from his brows.

"Nigga, I still say didn't nobody give the order to kill 'em, but fuck it, it's done now, and we can't do shit about it!" Tear stated as he just stared at the pistol sitting on the table.

"But look, first things first," he started as he just stared at Dough-Boy and then looked at Crazy Kev.

"What just happen can never be repeated by *nofucking body,* and once we finish counting this money, we gonna divide it three ways, and make sure it hit all three of our stash spots," Tear added, as the room got real quite and everybody just trapped their selves inside their own inner thoughts. It wasn't long before all you could hear was numbers being counted, along with the sound of Scarface voice coming out of the speakers of the television. All three men's heads were bowed; with stacks of money stationed in front of them, almost covering the whole table.

"Damn," was all Crazy Kev could say once they finished counting.

"Now, nigga, that's what real money look like," Dough-Boy added as he inhaled the smoke from the Newport he had just lit.

Tear stood to his feet, took a few steps backward and said, "$147,000," out loud, more to his self than anything, because Crazy Kev and Dough-Boy stood there monitoring his every move in anticipation and anxiety to see what he had in store for them next.

"Mann, I want you two niggas to know that we won't be one without the other. I really love you boyz, and it is a known fact that all we got is one another. We got twenty keys to get rid off, and the best way for us to do it is nice and slow, without a rush. But first!" Tear began, with an emotionless look written on his face as he walked back toward the table and leaned on it with both hands.

"We're taking a month off to let everything die down."

"But," Dough-boy said, before being cut off by Tear.

"But nothing, we ain't selling shit but rocks, and that's that. Do you hear me?" he added as he just stared at Dough-Boy, who wouldn't by any means put up a fight at a time like this with his Big Brother. He knew when to say something and when not to, and right now was one of those times that it was best not to say anything out of the ordinary.

"So in the mean time, what do we do?" Dough-Boy asked trying to figure out, just what else was to go with this.

"Look, we gonna act like we back to doing bad, we only severing smokers from here on out, and I'm ma go ask Fat Daddy to front me some work, saying our peoples down in the city Robbed us, knowing his big fat hating ass, gonn run and tell everybody in the streets that we came to him, broke, and begging for a hand out. And that's exactly what we want. So once the streets catch wind of that and begin to think that we broke, we just sit back and play our positions to the tee. Before you know it, the heat will be off us, and no one will even consider us for what went down today," Tear replied, as the room got quite and all they could hear were the sounds of their heart beating within their own body.

"By the time we finish pushing this work, it's a must that we have our retirement plan ready to be put into effect, because this game was only made to be use as a stepping stone, and step 1 is mission complete. Dats a wrap, baby. Step 2 is moving the work, and step 3 is staying close to the ground, off the radar, and out of these haterz way," Tear said as he rubbed his face as if he was real tried.

"Shid, that's cool with me," Dough boy said as he passed Crazy Kev the blunt, and leaned back in his recliner.

(CHAPTER 16)

A Cold Game It Is

1997

It was late the next day when both detectives came in. Sims glanced up from his desk as Jones strolled over. "What's up, my man?" He asked in a joking manner. And the two men grinned. "So how did the chief take your bait?"

"My bait, my ass," Sims replied. I told him it was our fucking idea, so he said to punch in. And we can pick up some overtime, baby! But he also said he don't want us bullshitting like it's our free time. So just as long as we get our fucking job done, he doesn't give a shit how much overtime we put in.

"That sounds all right with me. But how did the boys down in Narco take to the idea of us using one of their informants that's already locked up?" James inquired as he picked up a file from the desk and glanced through it.

Sims glanced at him. "It's not even necessary for us to go too far. Because they're going to call us down to their interrogation room for us to check out one of their men. They have a couple dope boyz on ice right now, waiting for us to see them. I was just waiting for you to come in. Because I figure you'd get plenty of rest and come in with that glow about yourself."

That's good buddy, because I needed that rest. "So where are we going to talk to our little stool pigeons? On Highway 6 or at the glasshouse?" James asked as he looked at his partner.

"We might as well drive to the glasshouse, because that's our next destination," Sims answered as he got up from his desk. "And plus I want to get a chance to see Ms. Simmons," he added as he gathered his jacket from off the arms of his chair.

James shrugged his shoulders in despair, "Well, let's get to going, because we have a whole day ahead of us. Hold on a minute, let me get the keys to the unmark," Sims stated as he went to the key rack and placed his chip in the hook the keys were hangin' from. Let's ride, baby boy, we got a case to solve," Sims said as he led the way out the side door of the department, and walked toward their unmarked police car. Both men rode in silence until they reached the garage of Waco's Federal Detention Center, better known to the public as the glasshouse, from the way it was built. Plexy glass windows were everywhere throughout the housing unit. And the inmates nicknamed it the glasshouse.

Both men exited the vehicle and headed through the double doors and made their way to speak to the guard at the counter. Then, they waited until the man went in the rear where the prisoners were held. There was a large steel door that separated the guards from the inmates. On one side was a room that the prisoners could talk with their lawyers in privacy. The room was not for visitors.

In a matter of minutes, the male guard was back. He had to wait until his partner opened the door from the control booth, allowing him to come back into the large room where they were seated. None of the guards were armed, and the two detectives had to check in their weapons before they were allowed beyond the garage. The guard was followed by an inmate name Tyrone Taylor, also known as Black Ty on the street. He was a tall, pitch-black, dark-skinned drug dealer, with a low haircut and a face full of facial hair from his stay in jail. He was silent, watching the developments quietly. He waited until the detectives grabbed him by the handcuffs and walked him into their interrogation room before saying anything.

"What's really going down, man?" he inquired in a cold voice, staring from one detective to the other.

"We just want to have a few words with you," Sims said softly, "because if you would like to help yourself, you can."

The man shrugged his shoulders. "Man I don't know what the fuck you talking about. I'm the wrong man for your job. I don't get down like that. So you can go fuck yourself, because I ain't no snitch, bitch! So take me back to my pod, before you two have to answer to my lawyer."

James let out a soft laugh. "Did anybody ask you about your dealings with the Hilltop Boys?" he asked as he glanced down at the brown folder he'd been carrying. "Tyrone Earl Taylor. Ain't dat your real name mister? Or should I call you Black Ty, the little man with the big problems?" The black man just looked over at Sims as if he was seeing him for the first time, and said, "ain't dat what dey got down here?"

Seeing that the man was going to the hostile, Sims spoke up. "Have a seat, Mr. Taylor. Would you care to have a cigarette?" He just ignored the outstretched pack of Newport's and reached for a butt in the ashtray to light it up. And that sent the message at once; he was going to be hard to get along with. "Now, Mr. Taylor, we didn't have you brought on here to bug you," Detective Sims began, "But we have a few questions we would like to ask you."

Taylor just stared at the detectives as if they were something of another world. "Listen, my man," he said in his cold matter-of-fact voice, "I know you guys got a whole lot of dudes who would be willing to answer all your questions, but it ain't like that with all of us. Every nigga in jail ain't your dime-dropping informants, so quit wasting your time with me, and go find that nigga that's willing to lead you in your right direction. Because I don't know shit, ain't heard shit, and I ain't seen shit. Now, do you two understand that?" he asked as he took a pull on the cigarette butt, and mashed it back in the ashtray. "Now, if you are finish with me, I would like to go back to my unit because I'm waiting for my bail hearing."

"Okay, that was your chance." Sims caught his partners eye and James slowly nodded his head. "Hey Dep," Sims called out, "Get this piece of shit out of here," he ordered as he handed the inmate over to the guard, He hated every fucking one of them smart-ass bastards that came off the streets with that "I ain't breaking my code of honor" attitude. "And could you bring me the other guy on the list?"

Taylor walked out without saying a word. He smiled at the deputy as he followed his step.

"Man some of them are like that," James said, tossing his hands in the air. "Maybe our next guy won't be so hard."

The detectives studied the folder of their next prisoner, Davis, Terry Davis. "He might just break. He got caught with enough dope on his case to be looking at fifteen years with five extra years for the gun possession," Sims said.

The other guard came forward, leading a short, dark-complexion man, who looked to be in his early twenties. He came in and searched the room with a turn of his head, and it was easy to see he was comfortable in this position.

"Hey man," he said as he took the seat that was offered to him. What's up with all this? Ya'll got me locked up on some bullshit, that dope nor that gun was mine. I was just giving this dude a ride, and when the laws stopped us, he tossed the dope and took out running."

"Yea, we know, Davis, we're going to help you too, only if you give us a little help," Sims said softly as he watched the man's leg start to shake. "Mr. Davis, if you help us, you'll be on your way to the house in the next few hours."

The mention of going home changed this man's feature. He smiled a smile that was like the sun breaking through on a rainy day. "A man, if I can help you, I'll do whatever I can," he said.

"Good, but don't give us no shit cuz we'll make sure Judge Jake Bernard slam your ass with twenty years Fed, and that will mean you won't see the streets until this time seventeen years from now. So do you hear me?" James said harshly, leaning in on the man, playing the role of a tough cop.

The man glanced over his shoulder as Detective James, and said, "Hey, man, why you want to give me a hard time? I ain't given you guys no problem, I'm I?"

"Who's your supplier?" Sims asked sharply, not giving him time to set himself. Davis began to shift around in his chair, and he mumbled a name under his breath. "It's this cat name Sub-Way," he said louder when James nudged him in the back.

"Sub-Way," he fired back.

"Yea." He's not from here, but he's been living here for about eight months now.

"Is that right," James asked, just as Sims butted back in.

"How does this dude sale his packs? Does he deliver it or do you go to his house?" Sims asked quickly.

"Naw, man," Davis answered slowly glancing around. "Hey, man, this shit can't leave this room because a nigga can get killed for saying as much as I've already said."

"Look man, don't worry about all that. This is an in-house secret. We just want to see if you're going to act nice or be an asshole," James replied.

"So how often do you re-up from this Sub-Way fellow?" Sims asked sharply. "Do you have his address?"

"Naw, man, he meets me at the Green Store (in front of Parkside on 6th Street), whenever I call him and put my order in."

And for the next hour, they had talked to the man, writing down all his information that would help the narcotics department but not them (the homicide division).

Finally, James put forth the question that they had been building up to, "So have you heard anything about the deaths of T'Meikco Johnson or Cocaine Wayne Thomas? I know you have an idea about who could have did it, so level out with us on it, right now, and we'll make sure that you get your freedom back as soon as we send word to the judge to sign your release."

Davis shook his head, "Man, that could be anybody. The word in here is dat it had to be a roberry. You know Cocaine Wayne was a big dude, moving keys for them Mexicans out of the Valley. So the best bet is to see if one of these local cats just pop up with big weight or to see if they just start spending money like crazy. Cause nine times out of ten, that's what's bound to happen," Davis added, as he glanced from one officer to the next. "That's the truth, but maybe I'll be some good help once I can change my vicinity."

The two detectives just looked at each other; sure he was telling the truth.

"Well, listen," Davis started, his voice holding a whining note, "If you guys put me back on the streets, I'll tell you what I'll do. I'll keep my ears to the streets. Ya'll just give me a number, and the first time I hear or see something, I'll get in touch with you guys. I got the ins and outs on a lot of boys that sale that dope, so look out for me, and I'll do whatever it takes to help you two bust this case wide the fuck open," he said as he looked at each officer as his words penetrated their minds.

James caught his partner's eye, and Sims gave him that nod of approval. This was all right with him, because each knew they could reap the benefit of having him in these streets.

"Listen Davis, if we do decide to cut you loose, don't give us no bullshit, because we will snatch your black ass back up any fucking time we feel like it. Now from the moment we let you go, we want to have you report to us on a weekly basis. Do you understand. By this time, next week, if we ain't heard from you, your ass will be right back in here. Do I make myself clear?" James said to the shaking man.

"I hear you, man. I'm on your team and I'm going to do everything I can to help ya'll." He just stared at Sims writing down a number and then passed it across to him.

"Here, this is our number, I'm Detective Sims and that's Detective James. And you better do what you say you gonna do because if your ass don't, we're gonna make sure your ass riot in jail, and your parole officer won't be born the day we sentence you to forever and a day."

James turned toward his partner, "A, buddy, do you want to go upfront and clear this matter for us, so we can get our man out on the streets?"

Sims just glanced down at Davis. "Yeah, I'll do it this fucking time, but this son of a bitch better produce a story for us," he said as he reached for the knob on the door.

Davis just looked at both detectives because he still couldn't believe his stroke of luck. And he couldn't wait to get back out there on the streets and clean this case up. His freedom was on the line, so he felt he had to do what he had to do to save his ass.

"So man if I help you guys out, what will be the outcome of this case I got?" he inquired in that whining ass voice of his.

Det. James just stared at the man. "Mr. Davis I want you to know, we'll do all we can to get you the best deal possible, but let's see how far you take care of your ends," he replied. "Because it's all on you and only you can control your destiny."

For a minute, Davis hesitated, then he slowly said, "Man, I'ma do what I can to help ya'll solve this murder, but don't leave me hanging when it comes to being there for me." And he dropped his head and folded his hands in his lap.

Sims walked back into the room. "Well, it's all taken care of. We're just waiting on the judge to send his authorization. It shouldn't take but a few minutes, then he can go."

Det. James just looked at Davis. "I hope you've listened to us, because like I said only you can control your on destiny," he stated, as the deputy knocked on the door and cracked it open. "We're ready for Mr. Davis."

And both detectives just watched their pigeon walk out, feeling and looking less of a man than he really was, but hey, they had a job to do, and each one hoped like hell that he do just what he say he could do.

(CHAPTER 17)

Live from Houston

Life after da roberry

The Residence Inn, Master Suite, was still dark as Dakota opened her eyes and got up from under the covers. The sunlight came flooding into the room as she pulled the curtains for the early morning Houston prediction. Tear just remained in bed, stretched out, watching the beauty of her complexion shining onto the ray of the sun. She was a nice mixture, if you were to let him tell it; Hispanic, African American, and Indian. She stood five feet four inches, with the body of a high school volleyball player. To him, her personality was what made her stand out from the rest of the females he has been with; since he moved back to Waco. Dakota was the only one that he felt comfortable around.

"Baby, do you me to wake your brother up?" she asked as she climbed across the bed and kissed him in the cheek. Tear just opened his eyes, trying to hide the fact he haven't had any sleep all night. "Please do, and check to see if he's hungry, because I'm starving like a muthafucker."

Okay, but first let me get you two an outfit out to wear," she replied, while her neatly manicured nails rubbed down his chest.

"Girl, you better stop before you start something you can't finish." She started blushing as she reached out and grabbed his early morning hard-on, while crawling off the king-size master bed backward. "See, that's the reason why your momma doesn't want us living with one another," he added as he grabbed his noticeable hard-on.

She smiled down on him. "Okay, Mr. Horseman, we'll see about that tonight. And I'ma make sure you call mommas name," she added walking out of the room to wake his baby brother.

Tear stayed still and glanced at the clock hanging on the wall. "Damn 7:52 a.m.," he said to himself. He listens and heard the exchanges between his baby brother and her. Well, it's time to get up because I have a lot of things to do today, and the thought of taking my girl along with my brother shopping was enough to make me remember the shape of my pocket.

However, today was one of those days where he had twenty-nine thousand dollars in cash to spend on whatever they wanted. And tha facts that he could care less about a price on the tag made him feel even more self-centered and swollen with pride. He had that right-now money, but anything outside of his pocket was only a phone call away, and that's what put a smile on his face. The only way to climb to the top was to use stepping stones to get there, and that's what kept him focused and determined to move forward in life.

"Tear, get out of bed, so we can go get breakfast," Rob called out from the doorway. He stood there silently and watched his big brother climb out of bed. "All right, lil pimping, give me a little time big head," Tear shot back as he put on his gym shorts and started walking toward the restroom. "Why don't you follow me knuckle head, so we can brush your grill," he added as he grabbed his lil soldier by the head and pulled him along.

For some reason, he felt good this morning. He usually got up and made his daily drop offs to his workers. But all this month, he didn't have to worry about all the stress that came with the dope game. He could spend time with his baby brother and his girl. And it felt good to be in his position; he had accomplished a lot to be only eighteen years old.

"Ry-Ry, what kind of shoes do you want for school?" Tear asked as they finished washing their faces. "I want some Jordans," he replied in an exciting voice.

Tear just grinned at his baby boy. "Well, I'ma see if we can get you some Jordans, but you got to promise me, you're going to be good in school with good grades. Do you hear me?" he asked as he looked at him through the mirror. "I promise." "We'll go ask Dakota if it's okay for me to buy you some school clothes too since we're down here in Houston."

Rob shook his head and turned his back and took off running. "Boy, stop that damn running," Tear called out with a smile in his face. He could hear his brother talking as he walked into the bedroom. Their clothes were all lying out on the bed neatly.

"Baby, did you send your brother to me for school clothing?" she asked when she walked into the room with him trailing behind her. "Yea, girl, you know I did, so what did you tell him?" he asked knowing she had agreed to it already. "Boy, you know what I said. I told him yea, if that's what he wanted," she added as she watched him get dressed. "Well, then I guess we got to get his lil ass some school clothes," he said as he winked at his baby brother. "Come on, Rob, let's let Ms. Fine Ass get dressed, we got to go chill in here for a minute," Tear added as he grabbed him by the head and pulled him along.

Within minutes, she was ready to go. "Tear, I'm ready," Dakota said as she came into the room. "Well, let's ride out," he replied and grabbed her by the hand and led her out the motel room with Ry-Ry close intact. They piled into the F-150, with Tear behind the steering wheel.

The drive to I-Hop didn't take long. They were all seated and ready to eat. The waiter was back with their order. It consisted of pancakes, eggs, pan sausages, and honey-butter toast. Tear has a steaming cup of coffee, while Dakota and Rob each had an orange juice. They ate in silence enjoying their small family gathering. Dakota watched the resemblances of the brothers, with a smile written on her face. However, she enjoyed being in the company of her man. His presence was enough to make her feel complete, and he was everything that she always wanted, but never really had; a thug with manners, and he was well respected by other gangsters that ran the streets of Waco.

"So around what time do we have to return these rental cars," she inquired as Tear washed down his food with his coffee. "We got until tomorrow but Tracie will take 'em back, but first, we have to find you a car to drive us back in," he added with a smile. "What kind of car?" she asked surprised to hear the news himself. "I guess, we'll have to see just what kind you like," he added as he grabbed her right hand and kissed it. "But first, let's go buy this boy some school clothes," He said as he got up. "Ry-Ry, get twenty dollars out of your pockets and leave it on the table." "Why I'ma do that for?" Rob shot back, not understanding what his brother meant. "We're leaving a tip because we're ballerz baby, and that's what ballerz do." And he placed the twenty-dollar bill on the table. "Yea, we ballerz," Ry-Ry added with a smile on his face. He loved both of his big brothers, and he wished he was there age because he wanted to go whereever they went. They always gave him whatever he asked for, but they wouldn't let him go in the hood 'cause they said it was too dangerous.

"Baby, I got the bill. You can go pull the truck upfront while I stand in this line," Tear asked as he let go of her hand.

"Okay," she replied, as she grabbed Rob by the hand and led him out the door.

"Damn," Tear exclaimed, stretching out in the passenger seat. "That food really hit the spot because I'm so full I can hardly move but I'm quite sure you can get us to Sharpstown Mall." he added as he reached over and patted her thigh. She just turned his way and smiled.

They all ended up staying in Houston for four days. Then, Tear decided it was time to head back to Waco. They had a nice minor vacation. They went Astroworld, everybody had bags of designer wear in the trunk of Dakota's 1995 Nissan Maxima Tear had purchased her. But now, it was time to figure out his next move. It was time to tighten up. They had a quiet trip back to Waco. Tear was deep in thought before he broke the silence.

"So did you enjoy yourself this week?" he asked as he pulled next to his mother's car in the driveway. "Yes, and you know, I did." "I wish we could have stayed longer, but I have to go back to work, and

I know you got things to do," she replied as they both got out and he picked his sleepy brother up from the backseat.

Everything was going just fine in her life, and she couldn't have asked for more, when it comes to the man who has just kissed her on her cheek told her he loved her, and blessed her with the opportunity to drive off in the car that he had just bought for her; the sweet smell of his Diesel cologne, da way he walk, da way he just blast out laughing when no one even knew what so fucking funny, with his bullshit ass joke telling ass, with all that lying and making everybody laugh, keeping the moment in full swing. But she had to respect the life that he lived; and she will, by all means.

(CHAPTER **18**)

Game Time

"Da Up's and *Down's*

It's been almost six months since I've been able to sleep right, but when I woke up on this one particular morning, I must admit, it felt good to be me.

I didn't have a worry in the world. I took a quick shower and a change of clothes. I was parking next to my brother and Crazy Kev.

Everybody was feeling the moment as we sat inside one our hideout houses and Dough-boy emptied the content of the shopping bag into the table. Not only were we moving the dope without a trace of being on the radar, but our plan was coming about just the way we predicted it to be. We were moving rock for rock on every brick, serving smokers any and everything—nickels, dimes, and twenties, along with fifty-dollar cookies that weighted a gram and a half. We were cutting a thousand dollars worth of rocks out of every ounce; pushing straight drop with no cut. And that had the crackheads going bananas.

"Twenty-seven thousand dollars," Dough-Boy said as three bundles of money came flying out the bag.

"That was this week rake in?" I asked.

"Yes, sir, it is," he replied. "It's been a drought on the streets, and the trap house on Lottie been off the meter," he added, just as Crazy Kev walked in and emptied his brown paper bag.

"Nigga, that's thirty-two racks right there, off my weekly rake in on Preston Street."

Money was all over the place. I had my stacks duct taped around my waist. We sat there joked and high sided as we all put our money up in our secret compartment. Everything was running smoothly. We had more money than we had ever seen. We were taking pictures holding stacks in our hands with stacks in our laps, smoking blunts, and enjoying life. The game was meant for us.

"Black Ty called and said the lawyer was handling the case pretty good," Crazy Kev said, as we sat at the table eating pizza. "That's good, I hope he beat that shit," Dough Boy replied. "Shid, he will. His lawyer is one of the best lawyers in Central Texas. So he'll be all right. He still can't get a bond?" I asked, looking at Crazy Kev.

"Naw'll, he said the state had a blue warrant on him for violation, so once he cleared all that shit up, he'll still have to go to the state for about six to nine months." "Oh yeah, I got a letter from Big Cuddy yesterday, and he said we were all approved to come visit him and that he'll be expecting to see us some time," Crazy Kev added in between bites of his pizza.

"Oh, yea, that's what's up," I began before adding, "I'ma call Dawn and see if she got to work this weekend, because she if don't, we can all go this weekend," I said excited about seeing one of our oldest cousins, who was still on lock, missing out on what life was really all about.

"Did he get that money and pictures?" Dough-Boy asked, as he got ready to roll up a blunt, pulling the weed out of his pocket, and breaking it down on the table.

"Yea, he got it."

"That's good."

"Oh yea, we need to go to Houston anyway and get with Dan-Dan about our cars. He called and said they'll be ready this Saturday."

"How much did he say he was charging us anyway?" I asked.

"Forty stacks for all three of them. And they fully equipped with the everything, except da swangers, but Lil Reno from Acre-Homes said he'd sale us # pair for ten stacks."

"Hell, yea!" Dough-boy added as he took a pull on the blunt he was smoking.

"And these boyz ain't ready, it's the summertime too. Mann, hold up! Crazy Kev explained as Dough-Boy passed him the blunt.

*   *   *

Everything was intact. Dawn had taken off from work. And we were all headed out to Sugar Land, Texas, right outside of Houston, to Central Unit, where our cousin Maine was being housed.

Here was the main piece missing to our puzzle. Our ghetto hero, the role model that we studied and looked up to and couldn't wait for him to touchdown and join us out here in the land of milk and honey.

If a person were to ask Big Cuddy a question about life, he'll make the same statement and answer your question at the same time.

"You pay to win, but you have to accept your loses too." And we all knew why he made that statement. He had lost two of his best friends to the streets since he's been gone; in which, he rarely talked about it, because it still hurt to a degree. It made realization set in, and he felt if he was home, they would have never happened the way it did.

But in these streets, you have to colt with reality and learn hard to survive regardless of the risk you might have to take, to get where you're trying to go.

Maine was like the modern, everyday gangstas that the media portrayed as a villain, but to us, he was our ghetto hero, never mind the newspaper articles about him, because to let the record reflect, almost none of them has ever stepped foot on a block that feed the mouths of almost 90 percent of every dysfunctional family, where drugs became the lifelines to keep the bills paid when McDonald's checks just didn't cut it and college took too long to payoff. The streets showed you the route to take, and like most young males, it teaches us to grow up faster than normal to go out and get it. But that was life for us, but we made it out and the game was being good to us.

As we walked into the visiting room, the sight made us feel trapped within the system, the sound of doors being slammed behind us. But it really didn't matter, because we were glad to get a chance to visit the missing piece to our puzzle. A live contact visit, not that five-minute collect-phone call bullshit, where he was only allowed to make {if he was on good behavior} every ninety days; and then, he called his mom's or his sister's. But we kept him with money on his books and pictures for him to see the world of long away from home that was basically it. If he needed anything else, he'd write and ask. By any means, we were always taught to look after our family and support them through out any of their problems.

We all had worn our "Free Maine" T-shirts, with a big picture of him on it. While sitting at a round table waiting for him to come out, we observed our surroundings, checking out other visitors laughing and talking about da latest dat done happened in the free world.

"There he goes," Dawn pointed as we all turned our heads to see Maine, a well-groomed, handsome young man, who prison had preserved over the years of good sleep and a healthy workout plan. In the streets, Maine had taken his time on the chin, like real gangsters do. With three years left, before he's eligible for parole on his thirty-four-year sentence, he was straight, because we all made sure of that. If he wrote and asked for us to send money somewhere for whatever reason, it was done without a hesitation; it has always been about the support of our family by any means.

Maine came to the table and hugged Dawn first, and gave us all hugs and playa handshakes, as we all sat down just looking at each other. It seemed like minutes had passed before the silence broke with laughter. He admired the T-shirts we all had on.

"Man, look at ya'll," Maine said with a smile on his face.

"Na'll, nigga, look at you with your big head ass," Dough-Boy said as we all started laughing again. We sat through three hours of good times and took lots of pictures. As we were getting more in depth with our enjoyment, a big, fat ass, red face correctional officer came in yelling, "Visiting hours is now over, so all inmates line up on the back wall, and all visitors move it toward the front. Do I make myself clear?"

Everyone brought closure to their visit and made their way toward the front. Kids were crying and running around, as wives, girlfriends, and family members waved. Kisses were being blown as I love you's were being spoken. We all threw deuces.

"Cuddy, we'll be waiting on you out here baby," I yelled out as the officer gave me a look that said, "Shut the fuck up." I smiled back, turned around, and threw the deuce again to my Big Cuddy, "Stay up boy," just as our names were being called to exit the visitor's room. That was an highlighted moment for all of us.

We all walked in silence back to Dawn's car, thinking about our Big Cuddy and how long he's been gone and how long before we'll be able to see him free again. Once inside the car, tears started coming down Dawn's face, we all knew it was because she misses her brother. Shid, we all miss 'em, but women are more sensitive than men are at times. In a man's body, he can hide the pain that his mind has taught it so well to hide. I guess it's because life will give you a lot of reasons to never expose your tears because the price you pay to show them is considered to be real experience. And the streets tell a man early in life, that a display of emotion is a sign of weakness.

But not for women, and we all understood her tears, because soon after that, she started laughing at herself and started driving, as we all fell asleep and arrived back in Houston about forty-five minutes later.

*   *   *

Houston had a record for having one of the most beautiful cities in the United States. The next day the sun was shining just right, hiding the clouds at times, then popping back out. Shining rays of light right down on the candy paint of the three '72 Buick convertibles, fully loaded with peanut butter guts with the ragtop to match. Crazy Kev's was wine-berry cherry dipped in silver, mine was do-do brown with twenty coats of glass, Dough Boy's was candy apple red, and they were stationed on the corner of Belfort and MLK.

All three of 'em had the fifth swanger hanging, belt buckles strapped across the trunk, the "World is Ours" was written in a neon light, showing every time we pop the trunk with the remote, exposing the screens tucked in the customized headrest falling from the visors and the well-hid speakers and amps. The PlayStation was customized to fit in the glove box, joysticks emerging from the lining of the seats. We paid Big Dan-Dan and called Reno and bowed all three on a glass set of fours.

We arrived back in Waco around five thirty that evening and decided to stop at the Shell gas station to fill up and ride our shit through the automatic carwash. The summertime and like any other town on Sunday, the park is off the chain, it's a spectacular event that all the local hustlers attend. In real tradition, you hustle all winter and shine all summer. And the park was a major social gathering and to bring the summer in like playaz do every year "Fish, Boochie, and Milly" threw a hood street birthday bar-b-que. These were three homeboys, whose birthdays fell on the same day, and they always did it big for the summer.

Everybody was there, females were out bopping, music being played, pictures being taken, and now heads being turned as we came through with all out tops halfway up, cocked in the air with Crazy Kev in the front, Dough-Boy in the middle, and me as the caboose as we swung from left to right driving slow, hiding behind designer shades.

"Man, who is that?"

"Girl, look."

"They can't be from down here!"

Then, Crazy Kev blocked and stopped traffic by turning his slab sideways taking up the whole street with his trunk popped, top dropped. He put it in park and got out; he grabbed a towel and a bottle of Black Magic Tire Shine and started spraying his Vogue's tire causing them to look shiny black. We all jumped out and shook hands.

"Girl, that's Crazy Kev, Dough Boy, and Tear!"

"Them boys did that"

"Can we ride with ya'll?"

"Tear, I see you boys."

We pulled up on the grass where everybody from the Eastside was. "Damn, my nigga, you boys came down this go-round," Boochie said as he came over as we were stepping out of our cars.

"Yea, baby, you know how it is. A nigga had to pull a stunt for the '97 summer? I said as I admired the sight of causing heads to turn. Fuck faces were everywhere and it's crazy how leather seats and candy paint make a hoe pussy get wetter than a melting ice cream.

"Damn, you act as if you can't call a bitch," a female voice said as a hand tapped me on my shoulder, while Boochie and I were talking. I turned around, and it was Candy, looking good in this hip hugging fitted dress that would give J. Lo a run for her money.

"Na'll, lil mama, it ain't even like that, a nigga been busy. Why? Wuz up with you?" I replied as I turned to face her and pitched her elbow.

"I guess, but what are your plans for tonight? Can I see you or what?" she asked without a worry of who could hear her; that's how it be when you're young and having money.

"I might, call me around nine and don't be late," I said, as she agreed and turned to walk off making her ass rock from side to side in rhythm motion. "Yeah, I'ma knock that off tonight," I said to myself as she disappeared behind the cars.

Once night started to fall, everybody gathered up and followed each other to Elm Street Store. The scene was crowded and it wasn't long before we all went our separate ways. I had a date, while Dough-Boy and Crazy Kev went to post up at our trap house.

*   *   *

The moment Candy opened the door, the blood started to flow in my body. The sight of her standing at the door in a pair of red stilettos, wearing only an opened robe that revealed a white Victoria's Secret teddy that stopped just above where her panties would've been, if she had been wearing any. The smell of a sweet fragrance filled the air as she let me in, closed, and locked the door behind me all while standing at the door provocatively. Candy was so overwhelmed that I came like I said I would. So she decided to put show on; dimming the lights as she sat me down on the couch and performed a little striptease. She straddled me facing me.

Even though me in jeans, I could feel the warmth of her body; sliding down grabbing her ankles, then turned around, and knelt between my legs. She started running her mouth down the print in my pants as she unzipped 'em. She pulled it out and licked the tip of the head before she ran her tongue along the rim. To my surprise, Candy took me deep in the depth of her throat like an old-school vet. Her lips were so soft and juicy that I almost popped, but then she turned on all fours and tooted her ass in the air and wiggled it, causing her ass to shake. She spread her legs out and reached between them starting to finger herself—finger sliding in and out of her pussy making it smack.

"You like that, don't you, Tear?" she asked as she threw her hair over her shoulder and looked at me in the eyes.

"It depends," I replied stroking myself.

Candy turned around and sat on the wood table and laid back. She spread her pussy lips with her fingers exposing her pearl tongue. I stepped out of my pants and straddled her with both legs on my shoulders, digging deep. She was tight, but I shoved myself inside her. She did everything but tell me to stop. I was punishing her pussy; then I had her legs spread like a "V" and was working out on her insides. We switched to a variety of different positions before my stomach got tied in a knot and shot my final load all over her stomach. We stayed on the couch and fell asleep, and I woke up sweating from a nightmare with Tameikco in it.

*　　*　　*

"Jerry, don't open dat door for nobody unless I tell you," Dough-Boy yelled from the kitchen. Jerry was the dope fiend that ran a twenty-four-hour trap house. In which, crack had da best of him, because his life only consisted of leaving his door open for anybody who would give him a hit of dope to use of his three bedrooms to fuck-suck and turn a trick in or to use his kitchen to cut or cook dope in. And those were the moments that he lived for, because dat meant the house man got extras.

"Come on Dough, let me get my hit first," he said as he stood at the door watching the chubby youngest cut a plate full of rocks.

"Man, let me finish this shit first, I got you!" Dough-Boy said with a blade in one hand and the other occupied holding the cookie in place, cutting it slice after slice, rock after rock. "All right, here, nigga, and don't ask me for shit else," he said taking two boulder size twenties and passing it to Jerry. "Now, let's go to work," Dough Boy added tossing two ounces of rocks into a sandwich bag. Da kitchen was a place that hadn't been eaten in; it was only used for manufacturing crack cocaine. Dirty dishes were piled up in the sink with trash lying on the countertop. The refrigerator only had two boxes of baking soda, a half gallon carton of spoiled milk, and a gallon of sink filled water in it. "Man, Jerry you need to get one of them dope fiend ass bitch to clean this bitch up," Dough-Boy said kickin' a Church's Chicken box as he walked to the living room; in which it was a duplicate of the kitchen, but a little bit cleaner.

"Knock, Knock."

"Who is it first?"

"It's Cher and Jackie."

"Let 'em in," Dough-Boy said as the two crack heads came through the door starching all on their face shit.

"What up Jerry, who here?" Cher asked as she walked her tall, skinny ass through the door. Before Jerry could answer, she said, "Dough-Boy, hey baby! Let me spend my thirty dollars." And Jackie jumped in, "I got fifteen dollars, Dough-Boy."

"All right shut the door," he said, while he pulled out three rocks, giving two to Cher and one to Jackie.

They passed him the money quickly and looked at Jerry.

"Can we go in the kitchen, Jerry. We'll give you a hit." Jackie said as she started walking toward the kitchen without waiting for his response.

Dough-Boy picked up his phone to call Crazy Kev. "Yea," he answered, sounding like his lungs were filled with smoke. "A, where you at?"

"I'm on my way right now, so make sure you got the money wrapped up right."

"I did that already, but stop by the store and get me a box of perfectos and a Big Red soda."

"All right," Crazy Kev added before the line went dead.

*   *   *

"Man, you can't just run in that trap house thinking Dough-Boy ain't got a strap. Nigga, you know, he's the damn fool out the click," Terry was informing Black-Baby, hoping he was listening.

"Nigga, fuck that nigga." I don't give a damn about none of them hoe ass niggas.

"You acting like a real bitch right now," Black-Baby shot back with his eyebrows arched up exposing his anger.

"You got me fucked up. It's fuck them niggas with me too," Terry replied hitting his chest to express the "me" part of his statement.

"That's all I'm saying. Then, we got to take care of our business when we get in there," he instructed as he pulled out a powder pack and ran his fingernail through it and scooped and snorted, all one motions, as he passed the pack to his partner in crime who had fired up a water stick and inhaled it, and immediate effect took place from the formaldehyde Newport that was dunked in PCP fluid as they both exited Black-Boy's '82 prime down two-door Cutlass and walked toward the trap house that they watch Dough-Boy go in about an hour ago.

*   *   *

"Cuddy, I got to make a stop and get that money from Dough-Boy before I ride out that way," Crazy Kev stated as right off Waco Drive, turning on Lottie.

"All right, but make sure you double-check everything before you lock it up," I said as I lay next to Candy on the couch exhausted.

"I got that down pack. I'll get at you first thing tomorrow," Crazy Kev added as he pressed the end button, tossing the phone in the passenger seat. "What are these two niggas doing walking around up here?" he said to himself when he passed two thugged-out looking black males in hooded sweaters just as a fiend was flagging him down, when she saw it was him.

"What's up, Sheila?" Crazy Kev asked as he rolled the window down, and she made an attempt to open the locked door.

"Let me in, I got three hundred dollars, but I need a good deal."

"You always want a deal," Crazy Kev said with a smirk on his face as he reached for his pill bottle and dumped eighteen rocks in his hand. "Let me see the money first and don't try none of that slick shit."

"Nigga, I always come correct," she said as she searched about nine pockets, all four of her pockets on the pants she had on and all four pockets on the shorts she had on under that, then her socks before she started to pull off her shoe.

"Don't pull your shoes off in here."

"I ain't, I know I got it." Finally, hitting her breast, reaching in her bra, she pulled out a nice stack, peeling off three hundred-dollar bills.

"I told you I had it. I just hid it from myself," she added smiling, "Man, Crazy Kev do me better than this," in a whining tone of voice.

"All right, here, now get your ass out my car," he added handing her another rock to seal the deal.

*   *   *

As Terry and Black-Baby made a way around the house, they were anticipating the plan that was about to unfold. Dough-Boy was there, and now, it was time to put in some work. "Bo-o-o-m," one kick to the door made the whole door comes off the hinges. Guns were out pointing at Dough-Boy, whose mind had froze and locked up on him; he dropped the blunt he was smoking.

"You bet not move," one gunman said as he stepped right in front of him, face hidden behind a mask.

"Set it all out nigga," the other masked gunman ordered, pointing a long ass old school 32 caliber revolver.

Not feeling the position he was in, his words got stuck in his throat, causing him to stutter. "Wh-a-what ya'll w-a-want?" Dough-Boy asked all shaky and shit.

"Bitch, you know what we came for, so let's stop spit-boxing and let a nigga get that," the first gunman said.

"Man, all I got is a stack or two in my back pocket, that's it."

"Turn around, nigga."

Dough-Boy hated that he said that because now his back was turned and he couldn't look these niggas in their eyes if he turned around. So he did what he was told as he felt the money being taken from his back pocket.

"Where's the work at," one said as he tapped the cold barrel of his pistol against Dough Boy's neck.

"It's under the vase over there, that's all I got, real."

"Shut up bitch," one said while the other one checked the vase.

"Damn, that's it nigga." The second gunman said to Black-Baby "this nigga lying," he stated not knowing he called out his partner's name, but neither one seemed to notice.

"What the fuck," Boow! Boow! Boow! Boow! Crazy Kev came in catching both gunmen by surprise. One gunman turned, but Crazy Kev beat him to the trigger, unloading the whole clip. Neither gunman was able to fire back once shots were fired. Dough-Boy jumped over the couch, taken one to the gut as the two gunman bodies dropped, and started shaking uncontrollably. Both men remained lying on the floor as Crazy Kev rushed over to assist Dough-Boy.

"Cuddy, I've been hit," he said in between breaths clinching his stomach.

"Damn, cuddy. Come on, we got to get you to a hospital!" Crazy Kev told Dough-Boy as both men stepped over the dead bodies and made it to the car. All Crazy Kev keep repeating was, "Hold on cuddy, we almost there. Damn man I didn't mean to shot you." His mind was so cloudy by the fact that he shot his cousin trying to protect him. All he kept saying was, "My bad, cuddy," as they rushed into Hillcrest Hospital Emergency, with blood everywhere.

"Cuddy, don't let me die," Dough-Boy was saying as the paramedics rushed toward both men, not knowing which one was the victim because of the amount of blood on both men. Women started screaming as four doctors were running down a hallway pushing a gurney. All of a sudden Dough-Boy blacked out and fainted.

(CHAPTER 19)

Things Just Ain't How
They Use to Be

Five Months Later

I pulled in front of McLennan County Jail, took a deep breath, parked, and got out. And for real, all I could think about as I rolled by myself in silence was how the time had finally came and turned the tables so fast in our life, where everything seems to have happen so fast, and I felt lost at times, without my brother at my side, but I made it my mission to do everything I could to hold them down by all means.

And once I made it inside, the first thought that crossed my mind was about all the visitor rooms I've been in since I was a little boy.

First, it was my daddy; then it was my uncles; and now, it's Dough-Boy, my own muthafucker brother. Life was taking us in a circle, and whenever someone made a decision to turn one corner, it was like they were destined to end right back where they started.

"May I have you ID," an older gray head, black correctional officer asked with an outreached hand. As I complied and stepped toward the back of the visitor room, waiting to see my little brother walk into a contained area to take a seat on the other side of a plex glass window. Just waiting made me think about when I will get my chance to on the other side of the situation; shid, we live the same life

I thought to myself as Dough-Boy strolled through a door wearing a county jail orange jumpsuit; smilin' once he seen it was me as he sat down at a booth, and I was given approval to go to booth three. We both snatched up the phone and waited until the CO hit the on switch for us to talk.

"What's up, baby boy? You all right?" I asked looking into my lil brother's eyes to make sure he was feeling a whole lot better since the last time I came to see him. Once he was released from the hospital, he was taken straight into police custody and charged with two counts of murder and possession with intent to deal cocaine. Everything happened so fast that when he arrived at the hospital, he still had two ounces of crack cocaine stuff deep inside his pocket that the robbers never got. His bail was set at one million dollars and bails bond man wanted $150,000, to get him out, but that would make the Fed's intervene. So he said he'll ride it out until it gets reduced.

"Yea, Big Bro, I'm chilling. I still catch sharp pains, but other than that I'm riding it out likes a G," Dough-Boy responded with a smile on his face. "What's been up with you out there?" he asked.

"You know everything still in rotation out here. It's kind of hard with you and Crazy Kev both being locked up," I said as I sat back a little bit in the seat I was sitting in. "I been fucking with Lil Juju and Young Chopper, letting them get their feet wet. Other than that, I'm holding down the fort all by myself," I added.

"What's up with Crazy Kev?"

"You know they only let immediate family visit at the Juvenile Centers, but Aunt Denise and Keyshawn went to his court hearing yesterday. The judge sentenced him to TYC (Texas Youth Commission) until he turned eighteen years old. He's straight. We have to get your shit situated. So what's the lawyer saying," I asked really caught up in the moment.

"Shid, he wants me to plea out to the dope, because he says that's going to stick without a doubt. But he say he's trying to persist a plea agreement to the DA to drop the murda charges to self defense."

"Yea, that's good then."

"He said he think I'll get ten years non-aggravated; so I'ma take that and get this shit over with. Everything straight though, just take care of everything. We'll all be out there together again soon."

"I can dig that, but nigga, I can't trust these niggas out here, so I ride solo and stay one deep for real. Oh yea, you know Dakota found out she was pregnant last month," I pronounced with excitement in my voice.

"Yea, so sister-in-law gonna bless me with a niece or nephew."

"Yea, she wants a girl, and I want a boy. We'll find out for sho of the gender in about two more months," I said changing the tone of our visit. I got some pictures I'ma send to you inside the car right now, so when I leave here I'ma stop at the store and take care of that. I've been meaning to do it but got sidetracked."

"You know, Black Ty was in the tank with me, but he got moved yesterday to another part of the jail."

"Yea, did ya'll get that money I sent last week," I asked.

"Yea, we got it."

"When you see that boy again, tell him I said to call me. I need to holla at him about something."

"All right, I'ma write him a short kite tonight."

For the remaining minutes, we continued talking, laughing, and going through certain plays that need to be handled. One thing I loved about my little brother was he never appeared to be worried about nothing. This nigga always seemed to keep his composure throughout all courses of our life. And at times, it's as if a lot of things didn't bother him.

"Man, I'ma come back next week, ya dig?" I was able to say before the CO disconnected our twenty minute plexy glass-phone visit and ordered all visitors to exit as they all shared the same exact expression on their face that said, "It's over already!"

Time just seemed to pass so fast when you're somewhere you want to be with someone you love and enjoy. Their comfort as a family member or as a soul mate/friend was within our comfort zone. It was a real touchy situation, but that's life I thought as I got up and me and my little brother threw one another the deuce, and I disappeared back down a long ass hallway all by myself.

As soon I drove off the premises, I did as promised, stopped by the post office, and mailed him those pictures with a short notation that read:

"Hold ya head up, because the rain doesn't fall forever."

One Love,
Big Bro

And I kept it trucking. I had a few stops to make before I went home and had a blockbuster night with my girl and a few of her homegirls.

Ever since Dough-Boy and Crazy Kev been on lock, she's been my confidant. I find comfort in her presence and the fact that she's pregnant has been a blessing to both of us. Both of our first born and all I could think about was her giving birth to a ten-pound eight-ounce mini me, and that alone eases my pain and fills my voids of missing my better half. But shit happens and the show must go on. I was a born hustla, a natural like the old playaz call it, and that's all I know; dope got to be sold and I got dope that got to be sold.

I heard the sound of Hot Boyz playing in the CD player as I made my way back to the block. And that visit made me feel more relaxed as I drove through a scene that I've known so well, the eastside of Waco, my home field, my hood, my turf, and the feeling of being in the hood is a feeling like none other.

My cell phone started to ring and brought me back to my train of thoughts as I picked up the phone.

"Yea."

"Tear, this Chopper."

"Talk to me, my nigga," I said remembering I was supposed to meet him earlier, but I decided to visit my brother.

"When can me and Jo catch up with you, baby,'" he asked waiting for my reply.

"My bad baby, I had to go visit Dough-Boy, but give me thirty minutes and I'ma meet you boys on the tail end of Lottie."

"Bet that, my nigga. I got that forty-three for you and Jo got his too, so we'll be posted up waiting on you."

"All right, give me about thirty," I said as I pressed the end button on the phone en route to go get them a re-up pack and pick up close to about nine thousand dollars they had waiting for me.

The sound of UGK was playing as I pulled in front of a trap house I've been operating out of with my two new recruits. I've been training them to get money on a larger scale, and they were doing as expected. Chopper came out the house followed by Lil Jo as one jumped in the front and the other one in the backseat of my car.

"What's up, Big Bro?" Chopped asked, being the more outspoken one of the two referring to me as his big brother. In the hood that term means more of a role model to the younger hustlaz who looks up to certain dudes in the game.

"I'm chilling, baby, but here's another nine-pack for each one of ya'll," I commented, as I handed each one a brown paper bag that contained nine ounces in it. They reached inside their pockets and counted out the remainder of the money they still owed on the last pack.

"Here's that money we'll be getting back with you once we finish with this pack," Chopper added as he turned around to get Jo money and handed it all to me.

"That's $8,700. That wraps up the last batch," he added as they exited my car. I recounted the money and pulled away from the curb. The digital clock on the dash read 2:45 p.m., so that meant I had a little time to roll around until Dakota got off work. I decided to go to the mall, just to walk around and buy a few things.

I came to a complete stop at the red light of Waco Drive and Valley Mills; when a Waco PD patrol car pulled up right behind me. All the while, my eyes were working the rearview mirror. The crooked ass white boy was running my plates, but I didn't panic; I was clean, without a worry. The light changed green. My foot then eased on the pedal, not wanting to hit the gas to hard and give him probable cause to pull me over. But out the blue the flashlights went to blinking and the siren went to screaming.

"Pull over," he yelled through the speakers. I was tripping; I haven't given this cracker a reason to pull me over.

"What the fuck is this hoe tripping on?" I asked myself out loud as I complained. I was clean. I had driver's license and insurance, so I figure this will only take a minute.

"What's the problem officer?" I asked in a shaky voice.

"Do you have identification on you sir?" A big ass redneck officer in a tight ass police suit asked. I handed him my driver license and insurance, and he walked back to his patrol car. About ten minutes later, he came back and he removed me from the car by placing me in handcuffs; saying something about I'm under arrest for a federal sealed indictment and started reading me my rights. But I knew he had the wrong guy.

Once we arrived at the U.S. Marshall's Office, I was fingerprinted and photographed. A nice looking, cute, white female came to the cell I was placed in and handed me a sheet of paper.

"Here's your indictment, Mr. Hilltop."

I couldn't believe it, I've never been caught selling drugs ever in my life, not even a weed case. And here it is my name, the first name at the top of this indictment along with Black Ty and two other niggas that I've never heard of or seen.

It read the "United States vs. Chance Hilltop." It was more like saying nigga it's you against the world, and my mind was cloudy with all type of thoughts.

"How in the fuck?"

"Who are these niggas?"

"This shit can't be real."

But it was. I was in custody, housed in the same county jail as my brother. To me, time was ticking slow and slower.

"C. Hilltop, you have a visit," the voice of a female came blurring hough the intercom, as I rolled out my bunk and freshen up. After five months of this shit, everything was starting to play out and gets old real quick. I was burned out on this shit.

Visits and letters is what kept a nigga sane outside of having my brother in the same tank with me and a few other homeboys we fucked within the streets. But someone special showing concerns and most of all feeling my pain to the same degree was something I never knew exited.

As I walked toward the visiting booth, I saw my pregnant Dakota smiling from ear to ear, stomach just poking out in her maternity nurse shrubs.

She picked up the phone with her well-manicured nails and took a seat waiting for the CO to turn the phone on. We sat face-to-face, eyeing one another, as she gave me that beautiful smile that I once cherished so much.

Dakota was willing to stand by my side through all that I've put her through, and she made that known from day one. Just then, all the inmates were seated and the officer hit the switch to cut the phone on.

"How are you doing cutie," I asked as I cleared my throat.

"I'm doing just fine, outside of the baby constantly kicking, making it hard for me to sleep."

"That's because he's a fighter like his daddy."

"Maybe like his uncle, because your ass ain't no fighter, and plus, who ever said the baby was a he."

"I did."

"Boy, you don't know shit, so how are things going."

"You know, all is well, just waiting to see how this shit turns out. Hopefully, it will be over soon."

"I know that's right, I can't wait either. How's Dough-Boy doing?"

"Shid, he straight, he was playing cards when I walk out the tank."

"Let him know I said Hi, when you go back in."

"I will, but when is the next doctor's appointment?" I asked as I switched phones from one ear to the other.

"In about two weeks, and Dr. Sparks said everything was looking just fine."

"That's good. Did you have the ultrasound yet?

"No, and I'm not, not now anyway."

"And why is that, why haven't you seen if it's a girl or boy?"

"Because I want it to be a surprise," she answered exposing her deep-rooted dimples.

"A surprise, girl, ya ass need to be buying all the right stuff, right now, as we speak."

"Okay, I will, but don't start all that. Now ain't the time, so what are they saying about the case?" she asked in a more serious tone, changing the mood of their voice.

"I'm sorry, cutie, but it's like this my lawyer said we have somebody snitching in our case, and they keep mentioning my name, and even though I've never been caught red-handed with drugs, their confidential informant word is more powerful in the eyes of the federal system.

"That shit just not right," she blurred out trying to hold in her composure.

"Babe, I know it's crazy, but he told me out of his own mouth that a trial is not the way to go."

"What," she yelled out.

"Babe, clam down and let me finish. He said that based on the 90 percent conviction rate tha FEDs have. But he's trying to figure out just how much evidence do they really have on me, so he can file for some kind of Motion to Discover."

"And what's that?" she asked as she begun to shake her legs.

"It's supposed to be a bunch of paperwork with whoever has written statements on me. In which, I don't know the other two dudes on this case. Shid, the only one I do know is Black Ty, and I doubt if he'll roll on me. So everything will be okay. I'll be home before you know it," I added as I cracked a smile and broke our eye contact and stared at the ground, because the thought of being in jail was nowhere near a comfort zone of mine. I couldn't even imagine doing no more than six months of this shit; this five months was killing me, but I was chilling, were the thoughts that crossed my mind as I looked back up, and our eyes locked in contact.

"Baby, don't worry or stress yourself, everything will be all right, and the Lord will guide us through all of this. And plus, you got me on your side. So it's a must we overcome all of this," Dakota spoke from the bottom of her heart as tears began to roll down her cheeks; just to see the man that she loved and cared so much about locked within a cage, like an animal, was ridiculous. This was her soon to be child's father, being trapped inside the system figure-four and expecting to go to prison, all because something his homeboy did.

"Baby, don't trip, everything will be okay, just mark my word," I said just as our visit was brought to an end. "I need you to do as I've asked, and stop being hardheaded," I said with a smile written on my face, as I just sat there and admired the way she looked sitting in her sit, ankles crossed, just staring at me through those glossy eyes of her. I couldn't believe it. Here it is, she's carrying our first born, inside of her, and I'm stationed behind a inch and a half thick plexy glass, draped up in jailhouse county blues, with a FED no-bond hold on me, not knowing if or when I'll be back home to support my family. But I couldn't let it stress me out. I had to lie in the bed that I made for myself. But that didn't stop us from enjoying the rest of our visit, laughing and high siding about the old times, when we were back in middle school, and it felt good to be in her presence. She made me complete, and she filled in all my voided areas, but to witness her walking out of those doors, always seemed to sap me back into reality.

"Chow Time," Dirty-Red yelled out, when he heard the sound of the trustees pushing food carts into pod.

"How was your visit?" Dough-Boy asked, as I laid on my back with my hands behind my head, staring at the pictures I had hanging above my bunk, wishing like hell I could jump inside and hold Dakota so close to me.

"Nigga, don't start all that damn stressing and shit," he said.

"Fuck you," I said as I rolled out of my bunk and took a sit on the edge. The same bullshit day in and day out, nasty ass food, stinky ass niggas with bad hygiene, and a whole bunch of lies coming from niggas just lying for the fuck of it, but it was their calm of fame.

"Mail Call!" Ms. Taylor yelled out, as she called the names of the lucky individuals who were fortune enough to receive mail from those that stood strong in their time of need.

"Mr. Chance Hilltop," she said in a soft tone of voice.

"That would be me," I said as I made my way from the back of tank.

"It's legal mail, so sign the log in book," she added as she handed me this 8 × 10 manila envelopes. I complied and made my way back to my bunk, sat down, opened it, and began to read.

"Nigga, what's dat," Dough-Boy asked as he sat next to me, as I continued to read in silence. I had just received my motion to discover, giving me all the evidence that the FEDs had on me.

At first, I was like these hoes ain't got shit on me, up until I came across some shit that would make a Lamborghini doing 180 miles per hour stop immediately at the slightest touch of the brake.

I must have read and read not really understanding a lot of it, but then the most shocking blow I've ever been hit with came into play. I reread it over and over, trying to see if I was reading this shit right. I couldn't believe it, my heart just dropped. I was loyal to that boy and this is how I get treated in return. My mind just froze at the statement as my eyes got watery. And read . . .

According to Tyrone Jamesone aka Black Ty, his supplier was Mr. Chance Hilltop. In whom, he would front him at least two to three ounces a day, and Mr. Jameson would pay Mr. Hilltop every night, and this went on for about four months on a continuous basis.

According to Tyrone Jamesone aka Black Ty, he would make runs to distribute crack cocaine throughout the Central Texas area, and the drug he got caught with came from his supplier Mr. Chance Hilltop.

According to Tyrone Jamesone aka Black Ty, the gun involved in the case was given to him by Mr. Chance Hilltop, to protect their investment making (money and drugs)

According to Tyrone Jamesone aka Black Ty, Mr. Hilltop is the supplier for the entire eastside of Waco, Texas.

I couldn't believe this shit. My eyes had to be playing tricks on me, I thought as I reread the statements over and over again. And after reading each statement, my heart skipped a beat each time, not really believing the words that my eyes laid upon. It was like watching the *real* transformations of my one and only top road dawgs turn snake right before the blink of an eye.

"Dough-Boy, Mann, look at this shit!" I yelled out and slung the paperwork into his hands, as he dropped his head and began to read it for his-self.

"Mann, this some hoe-ass shit, do you believe it? he asked as I felt myself in a space like trance.

"Nigga, my lawyer had told me that somebody on this case was working with the FEDs, signing statements against me, but he never said who it was."

"And it was this hoe-ass nigga the whole time!"

"I don't fucking believe this shit," I began as tears started to form in my eyes.

After all that I had done for this nigga, was all I kept saying and repeating to myself as I reread the statements over for the twentieth time; palms sweating from the anticipation, mind bogged with racing thoughts, and the only piece of hope I had, lived within the thoughts of not really wanting to believe this shit. But I couldn't take my eyes away from the ink that was already dried up on each sheet of paper.

1) According to Tyrone Jamesone, the crack that was found in this case was issued and supplied by Mr. Chance Hilltop (aka Tear); in whom, he has worked for ever since he was released from Texas Department of Correction.

2) According to Tyrone Jamesone, on February 9, 1998, he was instructed by Mr. Chance Hilltop (Tear) to transport and deliver a kilo and a half to (codefendant #1) Mr. Condre Malone, in whom counted out $26,250, dollars in cash and the purchase was then complete.

Tears formed within my eyelids as I continue to read, words just exploded on contact. Never in a million years would I have thought my own nigga would do me like this—a nigga that I had nothing but love for, one that I treated as if we were born and conceived by the same woman. Just then, I could feel a tear escaping from a place that I tried so hard to hide it. It did just what I didn't want it to do. Slid down my cheek and landed on my jailhouse pinstripe entire.

Life had taken my down a road that I never ever knew existed, up until I realized the difference between a friend and a foe. All type of thoughts ran through my mind. I couldn't eat; all I did was sleep and read the bible. Then one day I was lying on my bunk, legs crossed at the ankles, head propped up on the pillow, reading my bible, when I came across Matt. 26:23-28.

After I read verse 23, I understood what Jesus was saying when He spoke these words at his last supper.

"The one who has dipped his hands into this bowl with me will soon betray me."

And at that point in my life, I realized the mistake I had made, that had taken its course and turned fatal. Letting someone that I consider to be my ride or die potna penetrate the midst of my inner circle; in which, it cost a nigga ten years, eight months, and nineteen long ass days; of my life trapped within the system and hide, while behind a steel curtain, in a place where it's normal for those that love you to forget about you and leave you for dead, because you can't benefit them as long as you're away from these streets and locked up and hidden within the concrete walls of a prison cell; a place where you will soon witness the letters that stop coming, the visits that will reach the point of almost being un-heard of, and the unseen money that was sent, but never reached your account.

Life had took a turn for the worst, but though it all, I was still determined to walk out of these prison gates after ten long ass years; and do right by all means.

I'd be a damn fool to take myself through this shit again. It wasn't enough money in the world to push me back in that direction. I know

I was blessed in a whole lot of ways, and also I know there's more to life than what I had been exposed to. And it's plain and simple. Life had something in store for me, once I step foot out of these gates. And that's all that mattered to me.

*   *   *

"Pops, let me get one of them ice cream from you," Lil Ricky asked Pops as he were coming out of the commissary door.

"Listen to me, Lil Ricky, boy, begging will only make a bad hustla out of you," Pops said in response, always founding a way to use riddles in his everyday conversations.

"Lookout Pops, I'ma catch up with you later," I said as I laughed and tossed my commissary bag across my shoulder, to make it feel lighter from the weight of groceries that I had just purchased.

"All right, nephew, I'ma go head up way," he replied as we went our separate ways.

My mind was blogged from the extra five thousand I had on my books (commissary account). It was shocking to see an extra amount like that, just sent out of no where. Not that I was broke, or anything because I had money. It's not every day an inmate wakes up and finds that type of money sitting on their books without no way of knowing who sent it. So I made my way to our prison ATM machine, where all you do is insert your register number and your personal pin number, and it gives you all the information of your last forty money transactions, and as I did as I was instructed, I noticed that it was from my baby brother, in whom he was seven years old when I left the streets. Now, he's eighteen, and from the looks of things, he has come up on a nice piece of change, to be sending me five thousand dollars like that. I usually call and talk to him, but here lately, I've been planning for my release, trying to get my life back in perspective. Due to the fact that I have four months left and all I want to do is change my wrongs into rights.

On my way going back to my housing unit, I saw my two homeboys, Fish and O. Dee, en route toward the store to see if I was still there.

"Damn, nigga, you must of bust the store limit," O. Dee said referring to the amount of groceries that I had in my bag.

"Shit, I had to get a lot of shit this time," I stated as I placed the bag on the ground and searched for the two pints of ice cream that I had bought for them; in which, that's something we all did. Whoever went to the store, bought each one of us an ice cream. All three of us were partners in the streets, so it's all love between us.

"Here's the butter pecan and here's cookies and cream," I said as I handed each one their ice cream. "Where ya'll going?" I asked as I tossed the bag back over my shoulder.

"We'll be on the rec yard," Fish said as O. Dee's mouth was full of ice cream.

"I'll be out there on the next move as I put this shit up," I said as I made my way up the ram en route to the Austin Unit. The correctional officer Twin Mac, an older white male, called my name as I was about to pass him. "Mr. Hilltop, you got mail, wait by my door I'll be right in."

"All right," I said just thinking about who could have wrote me this week. A letter is so valuable to a person who is trapped within these boundaries. It gives us something to look forward to, let us know we're not alone on this ride; it gives the soul a burst of energy, and it delivers strengths to the spirit of the weakest of any man or woman under this condition. I've been fortunate enough to have certain people stay down with me the whole time I've been in prison. Only three rode the whole time, when some rode halfway and then jumped out, while others jumped in halfway and rode it all the way out. In which, I do appreciate every minute a person has invested in lifting me up during times like this. Eleven years is a long ass time, so it's understandable if the ride was too steep to climb, I can dig it.

"Here, boy, you got a lot of love today," the cool CO said as he handed me four individual letters and packages of pictures.

"You know how it is when you get short on time and everybody is anticipating the moment you walk out of these gates," I replied with a smirk on my face as I made my way to the cell. I guess my celly was out on the yard somewhere. I placed the commissary bag on top of the stationary locker and sat down at my desk, and opened my first letter from Tan, my new fiancé.

> Hey Babe,
>
> I'm sitting here counting down the days, waiting for the day I see my baby walk out of those gates of hell. It's been a long time coming, and now we're four months away from living our dreams. I've been shopping, and I found a few more outfits that I know you would like. Chance, I know I've only been in your life for seven years, but babe, I wish I could have been your rock of comfort for the entire eleven years, but I do feel that we were meant to be apart of one another. Oh, and I searched online and I found a great location for the barbershop that you want. So once you get out, we'll go check into it, and if it's right, we'll get it "Okay." It's getting late and I have to get up early for the week. I love you babe. Call me when you receive this letter, and don't forget I'll be down there for visit on Sunday. So be ready and don't take your precious time. I'll write back soon.
>
> Love Always,
> Yours Truly
> Tan

It felt good reading her letter, because she always finds a way to lift my spirits and let me know she got my back. She stood her ground for seven years flat, and we met each other through mutual friends and she became the rose that grew through concrete. The next letter I opened was from my mom's and just the sight of her handwriting can make me feel like a little boy again, the only woman in my life that can do me no wrong. I smiled as I opened her letter.

Mr. Chance Hilltop,

My first born, my night and shining armor. How are you doing handsome? I hope my love was able to find you standing firm on solid grounds. Well, as for myself, I'm patiently waiting for my baby boy to finally come home. It's been eleven years and I've felt every last one of them without you in my presence. I'm glad you have your mind on the right track when you're released. Somebody needs to talk to your baby brother. He just don't listen. He's out here doing the same things you were doing. Him and Dough-Boy are back at it again. Son, I hope you don't come home and jump into that deadly game. Why can't ya'll see that no one has won in that game; every one has taken a lost, rather it be mentally or physically. The money is good, but it's only momentarily, existing only for a short period of time. Son, think beyond the moment, you have to plan for the future. Your son needs his father out here active, regardless of what you and Dakota have went through; she's only human, and being of that nature, we're all entitled to make our own decision, rather than in your favor or not. So baby, come home and do the right thing; learn from your mistakes, don't continue to make the same mistakes. Think about it, how many eleven year bids can a person do in one lifetime? Ask your self that. I love you baby and I want the best to happen in the near future. I'm proud of you son, regardless, always have been.

Love,
Mommy Dearest

My momma always spoke her mind, and she was always the one to accept me for me, and tried to help me make the right decisions. Me being me just made bad choices on my own. She did the best job that a mother could do, by raising us to be respectable children, with well manners. I hate that the impact of my poor decision making affect my mother. I folded her letter and placed it on the desk, and opened the next notation. It was a short letter from my two brothers, Dough-Boy and Rae-Rae. That was shocking because these niggas never write; so I opened it and read it

Big Bro,

What's up with it, baby? I just touched back down, and the street's lovely baby, everybody is out. (Me, Maine, Crazy Kev, Dee-Wee, and Baby Bro. In which, you know this nigga name done changed. The streets call him Baby Face. He looks like a split image of you, even act like you too with that bullshit ass laugh. Big Bro, every thing was still put up the way it was left. So we still running the same plays like ninety-seven. Baby Bro is doing it big, baby, this nigga one for real knee-deep in the snow, birds flying south for the winter. He said to call him and that he sent five stacks to your books, so that should be there by now. Big Bro, you're the only piece missing to the puzzle right now. But don't trip; we got you right when you come home. I'm pushing that Lex 430, pearl white, twenty-two inch blades, chopping these boys up out here. Baby Bro, knocked off the Range Rover last week and that bitch nasty, he got that bitch buttoned up on twenty-four's with seventeen inch screens. It's platinum gray wrecking the screen. Maine, Crazy Kev, and Dee-Wee, all got black-on-black Dodge Chargers. Big Bro, the streets are lovely out here. We just sitting back waiting on The Don to come home.

One Love,
That Boy

And that's just the way it be. When life comes at you from all angles, the Game is like a pool of snakes, the wrong choose you fall prey to one of the most deadly snakes of them all, your own kind, the one that pretend to be what he ain't. So who's your friend and who's your foe. I never knew, but my family is all I got; me, my brothers, and my cousins.

CHAPTER 20

One Month Left

It's Been a Long Time Coming

"Young brothers, mark my word, because the words that I am about to speak were chosen by the Lord himself, and I must admit you know like I know, that without him there's no me nor you." Rev. Dollar Bill began the moment he stepped to the podium, wiping his forehead with his signature pearl white face towel, as he placed the wireless microphone in the midst of his right palm.

Here was a man, who has been through a whole lot in what we call this day and age; in which, the Good Lord has called upon him to preach his word to those that needed to hear his message. And believe me, the highly intelligent Rev. Dollar Bill had a way with words; and he made it his mission to get his point across to you as you came to understand and vision the message that the Lord had sent him to teach and deliver.

"However!" he began. "Sometimes, it's the smallest things in life that can really teach us a very valuable lesson; only if we would pay close attention to the detail and take heed to the signs that warns us because there's not a man in here that can say warning didn't come before destruction. Rather if it came in the form of a dream or in the form of you overlooking reality; such as the ones we once called our so-called friends, the same ones that could care less if we ever see the streets again—our homeboys, our playa potnaz, your ace in the hole, and even the ones that you once consider to be your family," he said as he took a long pause and looked around at each and every individual.

"Faces don't lie, they hide behind frowns and smiles, and I'm willing to bet that over half of us within this room have been and went through some of the same exact situations, only with different details but the same subject topic."

The Chapel of the Federal Correction Institution in Bastrop, Texas, was once again jam-packed; inmates were everywhere; all the seats were filled, people were standing; and all ears were tuned in to hear every word that escaped the mouth of the Rev. Dollar Bill, a mentor to his peers, and a wise man of true meaning.

"Listen to me and listen to me good, my brothers, never ever judge a book by its cover. Because we all know looks can be deceiving. And if you don't just take a good look around this very room that you're sitting in," he added as heads began to turn and eyes began to roam.

"In this room, we're all guilty of falling short of our own true glory, but who do you blame. Do you blame the system that we grew up in, the section eight housing projects, or the drug-infected corners that go hand in hand with our past. Or tell me this, do we blame our parents for giving us their all, rather if it was enough in our eyes or not. Or do we blame the family and so-called friends that let us down the day we were captured and held hostage without a bond," he added as he paused and took a good look at almost every individual that was in a state of giving him their undivided attention; because what he was saying was really making a lot of sense.

"My young brothers, don't live the rest of your life blaming other people for your mistakes. Because, in reality, you're the captain of your ship, and I advise every last one of you all to only blame yourself if your ship wreck, regardless of whoever plays a major role in your future or past downfalls. However, it was you who made the final decision of dealing with that person, rather if it was out of love or another apparent reason. It was you and your thought process that brought about your own fatal downfall. But right now, I want you to understand that now is the time for you to open your eyes and realize that change is a suitable thing for all of us. Yes, it will be a proven fact that a rough transition will come and follow each and every last one of us, the moment we walk out of these prison gates. But my main focus is to inform you that: The Lord has a plan for all of us."

And at that moment, quietness filled the air, as Rev. Dollar Bill pasted from side to side, with his eyes drawn on no one in particular; but all eyes were glued on him. In which, the Rev. Dollar Bill was a retired hustler in whom has turned his entire life around for the Lord, and did away with all his old devilish ways. He was a real good dude, and you could tell by the way that he carried himself, that he was one of those dudes that was a walking billboard for all that has ever heard of him and all the million-dollar storyies that followed him.

In which, it was once said that he lost millions and went broke back in 1988, but was back on top of the world with twice the amount or money by 1989. Even though he never bossed or bragged about his past, but every now and then, magazines would print articles about him and how he played a major role in the drug trade that became widespread throughout every ghetto in America.

"Now, young brothers, I want you all to know that growing up I was a brave little boy, smiling during some of the roughest times in my life, and believe me, we had some rough times in my day and age. Our values were a whole lot different back then too. Even though money was hard to come by, my mother used to always find a way to put food on our table. And to me, that meant a lot. However, to be without food for the most part of the day, it felt good to finally get a chance to eat almost anything. And my mom was one of those mothers that would serve us right before it was time for us to go to sleep, and then tuck us all under some of the best passed-down blankets any single mother could find.

My daddy had to be a deadbeat, because all I really knew was his name. But to be born without one was normal, and not only for me, but most of my friends lived without a father figure, so it didn't faze us. You had to be there for your other sibling, and make the best of it." Rev Dollar Bill stated as a smile crossed his face and he just stared at the ceiling and began.

"To me, those were the days, and my life really had a meaning to it. Not only was I focused to find my place in this world, using my brain to figure things out, but I had no other choice regardless of if I wanted to or not. At times, I knew beforehand, if my mother couldn't provide food for me and my siblings, all I had to do was open the refrigerator, and it would tell me all I needed to know." You can tell Rev. Dollar Bill was trapped in his own little world as he drew a picture of his priceless moments.

"If there was next to nothing and almost empty, that meant our late-night dinner would be a five-pound bag of white rice mixed with butter and sugar, a loaf of bread, and a nice glass of ice-cold hydrant water. And it wasn't long before I did just what almost every kid my age did, promised myself that my momma wouldn't have to struggle like this if it was left up to me. And from that moment on, my mind was made up. My mission was to turn all my nothing into something. And being born with a whole lot of nothing didn't take much to make a small amount seem like a lot, and life seen within my full reach. I became a product of my environment and didn't even know it, because everything I did was normal to me; but it took a long prison term for me to really get a clearer vision on the real values of what life really is," he spoke as he wiped his forehead and gripped the microphone even tighter.

"We have to be open for change. A person can't be set in their own ways of thinking without giving everything a brief actual breakdown. Because if we all did just that, that will only mean that we're not willing to try something new. You have to approach life from a different angle and adapt to legitimizing everything around you. Whereas every time the Lord, our God, opens a door for you, it's your opportunity to move forward, and you have to be an opportunist. A change is a turning point, and we all need freshness in our life. You can't be worried about not being used to it, because those are the thoughts of the devil working to keep you from maximizing your full potential. And those thoughts are the thoughts that are pulling you away from moving forward; not realizing that's your main downfall.

The Lord will bring about new opportunities but it's just up to you to take full advantage of them once they cross your path. Here it is in the near future, some of us will be faced with a position that we'll feel is well above our head; when in reality, it's not. We're just used to being stuck in a one-track mind; in which, there will be some of us who will have an opportunity to change careers, but won't, because they don't know their self-worth. You are your value point; you just have to be able to widen your horizon. If you really want to experience the best the Lord has to offer you, you have to be willing to take risks, and step out on faith. You will have to be open to new ideas, when they come across your path. Just don't find yourself being clos-minded, thinking something new is not for you. God has a plan for you and, yesterday is just what it is; past tense. You can't live your life on your yesterday's victories because they don't count; it's in the past, because we're all living for the future. I know it's a lot of us, and I do mean us; because I've done it before, that sit back and day dream about the good old days. But I'm here to inform you that the *Good Lord* has something new in store for you and I. Yes, it is a true statement that over half of us were raised in dysfunctional homes, with no one to really give us proper guidance. However, our role models didn't have a sense of direction, so how do we go about living life following in their footsteps. That's like the blind leading the blind. There is no way possible for them to lead us to the well to drink water, and now, that I've had the chance to sit back and analyze my life, I realize how limited I was in my one dimensional way of thinking. So at this moment, I want you to think about reinventing yourself, get a new vision for your life, you have a gift and you have something to offer.

You wouldn't be here if God didn't have something great for you to accomplish. Put yourself in the right environment, and don't get stuck with the mind-set that that's all you know how to do for the rest of your life. Then, you'll begin to see God open up new doors and keep looking for new opportunities, be willing to get out of your comfort zone. Start starching yourself; you have to stir up what God has put on the inside. Because if you don't have a dream, you're not really living; you're just existing; and you have to have a reason to get out of bed every morning. Find something that you're passionate about, something that you want to accomplish. So to make a long story short, stay open to change. You can't let one disappointment or even a series of disappointments convince you that it's not going to happen. You may try and fail, but understand that failure is not a denial, it's just a delay. In which, each every last one of us are entrepreneurs in our own form or fashion.

Rev. Dollar Bill added as he stepped away from the podium and his glance came to a long, hard, deep stare, as he was brought back to the harsh state of reality, and his voice became a cracking whisper.

"Please bow your heads for a moment as we come together and adjoin one another in prayer."

However, the prayer brought about and ended with a strong thick "Amen," as not one person was ready for the seminar to end. It was as if the reverend had all the answers to our questions, and he could motivate you to look within and find the person you've been searching for all your life. "You."

*   *   *

The moment my homeboy Ko-Jack seen Rev. Dollar Bill after last Sunday's service; it was as if he was so anxious to approach him, because all he kept saying was, "I need to talk to the reverend before I walk out of the place next week."

"Well, call him over here, and stop saying the same thing over and over again," I said as we passed Austin unit and seen the reverend speaking with Young Marco from Killeen, Texas; in which, their conversation was coming to an end as we begun to walk toward them.

"A there, young fellows. How are you guys doing today?" he asked with an outreached hand, once he seen us coming in his direction.

"We're just fine, was basically trying to get a moment of your time. That's about it," I said as we all exchanged handshakes and stood in the shaded area in front of the unit. And within moments our conversation was shifted into a real eye-opener.

"Ko-Jack, people will try to discourage you from reaching out for your blessing, you just have to always remember. You have to come to your closed doors before you're ever going to get to your open doors. Sometime you will run into ten people who will tell you 'no', before you come in contact with that one 'yes'. You just have to believe in the Good Lord our God, because, for real, you wouldn't be alive if He didn't have a purpose or a dream for you. God knew every disappointment you went through before you went through it, he has always had the solution before you had the problem."

"But Rev, I'm destined to be released next week and after six years of being in prison, all I really know how to do is sale drugs to get me were I need to be."

"Young brother, let me tell you something. You are way smarter thea you think, because you have a gift, and on top of that, you have something to offer the world. So don't fool yourself or sale yourself short, because if you can sale drugs you can sale stocks and bonds. You can sale electrics, you can sale medical supplies. All you have to do is get a new vision and reinvent yourself. Don't use your god-given talents for all the wrong reasons. Just think about it, we all have sold drugs in some of the roughest neighbor-hood in this world, and that only means we all have the gift of grab, because for one we all had the strategies of a Fortune 500 company. Use your head and don't set yourself up for failure, because in order to sale drugs.

You have to know how to market your product, and that's *marketing*.

You have to know how to get the word out, and that's *advertising*.

You have to know how to treat and take care of your clients, and that's *customer service*.

You have to know when to sale and when not to sale, and that takes a *manager's decision*.

So don't tell me that's all you know how to do, because it's not, and only you can bring yourself down. In which, your mind has to be made up well before you walk out of these gates. I know both of you two are about to walk out of this place. I've sat back and watched you two as long as I can remember and admire the friendship you two have. But it takes one of you to help lead the other in the right direction. Because unlike you two, I don't have a release date; but to witness each one of you walk out is enough for me. My word will walk out of these doors, and I hope you all plant the seed within your soul and harvest the blessing the Good Lord have in store for you."

At that moment, I realized the Rev was a lifer and would not see the streets again. Here it is, I'm complaining about the ten years I've done and Ko-jack whining about the 6 years he has done; when in reality, the reverend was content with living his life and watching inmates be released, hoping someone would take full advantage of what freedom really is.

You are free to make your own decision, and you are free to ruin your own life. It's just up to the one in whom you face whenever you take a good look in the mirror.

"Young fellows, all I want you guys to know is that life is reality and *It's all on you.*"

To be continued:
-Part 2

"We all We got"
"Just like my oldest brothers"

A story where Baby Face
(the youngest brother) comes into play
with his mind on a mission;
to overcome any obstacle that stands in
his way. Just like his oldest brothers.